# ALLAKAZZAM!

**A Novel**
**&**
**Three Short Stories**

## DANIEL ABELMAN

BeWrite Books

Published internationally by BeWrite Books, UK.
32 Bryn Road South, Wigan, Lancashire, WN4 8QR.



A CIP catalogue record for this book is available from the British Library

ISBN: 978-1-905202-28-7

Also available in eBook format.

Produced by BeWrite Books
www.bewrite.net

Bd's

The only person I have to thank for this book is my beautiful wife, Joani, who from the outset showed minimal interest. But she also gave me incentive and encouragement by repeatedly telling me I would be doing far better in finishing off the bathroom: "It's been nine months already – I'm bringing in a contractor."

I love her like a rock.

# CONTENTS

# ALLAKAZZAM!

# CHAPTER ONE

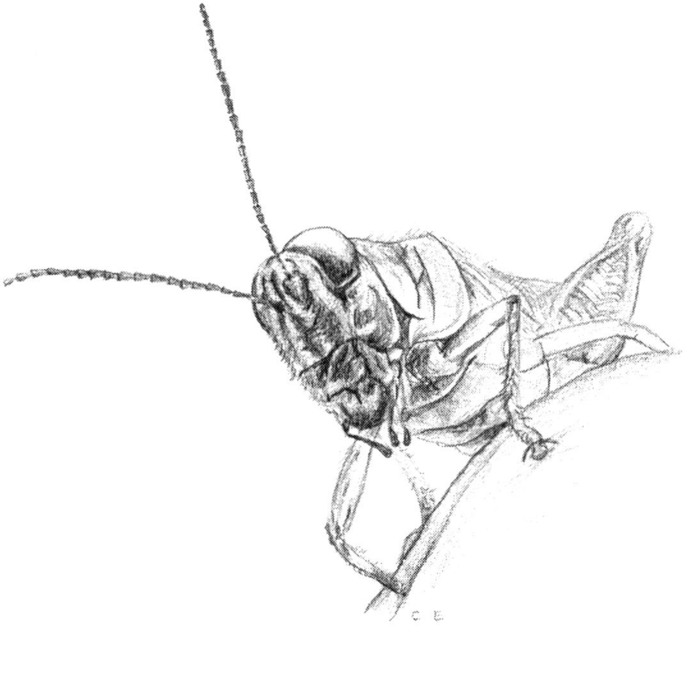

*"Ngubani igama lakho Sissie? What is your name sister?"*

*"No More Daughters, my chief."*

*"What number were you, sister?"*

*"Four, my chief."*

*"And did the magic work? Who was the witch doctor?"*

*"Yes, my chief, it worked well. UmZealie was his name."*

*"Huaw! Old Four Legs is still alive. So you come from the*

*place where the five cows died, my sister?"*

*"Yes, my chief. I was born the year the rains came twice."*

*"Your Aunty Zena was my wet nurse."*

She realized who I was.

*"I see you, my brother HardSucker."*

*"I see you, my sister No More Daughters."*

*"Aunty Zena got me this job. She used to work here; before the Old Madam died."*

*"What are these papers you carry, my sister?"*

*"A boy that looked like a man brought them, my brother."*

*"What did he say?"*

*"He said he was Tokoloshie, the son of Tokolosh, and if I did not give the Master these papers he would come back again, riding a hyena."*

*"How did he come this time?"*

*"He drove a car."*

*"And what did you tell him?"*

*"I gave him a bonsella one-bob and told him to hamba."*

*"And you gave it to the Master?"*

*"The Master came home and asked for some papers, so I gave them to him."*

*"You did well, my sister. Do not tell anyone about this."*

*"No, my brother. I am like the baboon who can only count to three."*

*"I will come on Sunday, when the Madam is out, and you can make some samp with beans for me in the pressure cooker."*

*"I see you my brother HardSucker."*

*"I see you my sister No More Daughters."*

She curtsied vaguely and scurried out of the room.

Freddy broke the astounded silence evoked by a white man conversing in Xhosa.

"I see you speak in tongue, old boy. But what did she say?"

"Absolutely nothing. She knows nothing at all."

"But she said 'yes' when I asked her if she had any idea where the manuscript came from," interjected Madam, the hostess of this unexpectedly engaging soirée.

I repressed a long sigh. “Your maid comes from a good family and is extremely well mannered. She would never be so impolite as to answer ‘no’ to your question, especially in front of all these people. If you asked her whether she could walk a tightrope, she would’ve answered ‘yes, Madam’.”

I turned to Freddy. “What she did tell me, though, was that you and I are brothers of sorts. It turns out the woman responsible for your personal hygiene was the same woman who taught me the Xhosa language. I was brought up on a farm and *Aunty* Zena was more than a mother to me.”

Madam erupted a jubilant shriek. “Then we’re family! Maybe I’ve inherited psychic powers from the same place you got them. I wondered where I got my clairvoyant gift …”

“What are we going to do?” bulldozed Stephen.

You didn’t have to be psychic to guess Freddy was going to suggest they ask a psychic. But Madam jumped the gun by proposing that I be the one to track down the missing parts of the manuscript.

The Master and Stephen wearily agreed to fit the bill if I could prove I actually possessed some psychic aptitude. So, right then and there, I converted Freddy from a skeptic into a believer by reading his very mind. Proof enough.

Armed with a fax copy of the manuscript, together with an appointment to discuss terms at Master’s publishing company with Master and Stephen, I took my leave of them.

“’Bye, all. *I see you, my brother Freddy.*”

# CHAPTER TWO

Contrary to popular belief, psychics need a lot of sleep, so when I arrived home, tired from dinner and dessert of extrasensory demonstrations, I quickly made sure that all the windows and doors were latched and locked. Finished with my security check, I washed my face, gave my teeth a good brushing and then, after I made my final pee, I jumped into bed with the manuscript. I would have preferred to jump into bed with my wife but she had left me years before.

Having promised Stephen that I would at least look at it before our dawn meeting, I thumbed through the stack of papers. The manuscript, handwritten in hazy fax-machine gray, would not be easy to read, especially as the edges of the sheets kept curling up. With a random flip, which brought me to an inside chapter, I snuggled down for a quick read before I crashed out:

## The old?
## *I plan a putsch*

Every body has a unique odor. Ask any bloodhound and he'll tell you that your body's metabolism intermittently releases imperceptible amounts of gas into the atmosphere. As you bounce down steps, the undetected whiffs work their way out — by all accounts, indiscernibly. But let the truth be told: those whiffs cling. If you eat curry for three days you'll smell like an Indian, whether you like it or not.

As I would be going into the Township in the disguise of an Indian cut man to provide expert first aid to the cuts and bruises of the combatants during their fisticuffs, days were spent sleeping on the open patio letting the sun burn away any signs of my breeding, as nights were spent cooking up curries. I was going to a hot place and if the smell of my sweat did not have an Indian's signature – if I did not smell the part – my complexion and accent alone would not suffice. The TzotziBoys would sniff me out and turn the whole affair into a messy, one man Coon Carnival.

The TzotziBoys Gang ran the Township. It was a horrid, horrible place with trouserless picaneen; their foreskins dusty in the summer and their lower faces caked with dried snot in the winter. The dust and snot of the *sans culottes'* formative years could only be washed off with water from the tap; to which it was a five minute, heat dazed walk in the summer and a three minute slosh through mud in the winter. It was shared with many other shanty home *pondokies*; but it was one of the TzotziBoys Gang, irrespective of the season, be it winter or summer, who controlled the tap's brass butterfly handle and its low-pressure drizzle.

If he told you '*hamba wena*' then you would 'scat' and postpone attempting to wash the snot off your face for a day or two before you tried again. Or listlessly wait until your mother, relieved from her duties as a domestic servant on the other side, came home for the weekend. She could then dole out a ticky coin from her pay of two-shillings-and-sixpence to give to the TzotziBoy who was on tap duty; paying for your right to squat under the tap and take your weekly shower whether you needed it or not.

With so many maids home for Friday night, listlessness as the order of the day was rescinded, with the TzotziBoys imposing revelry in an attempt to elevate the economy and knuckledust the Township out of its fiscal slump. Selling water rights during the week and various revelry rights over the weekend would, or should, have set the TzotziBoys up for life, had it not been for the Bakateeny HardTimeBoys Gang.

The Bakateeny HardTimeBoys Gang was making a play for power and I, having masterminded the escapade, was going to be in on it.

One generation back, Queeny Bakateeny was robbed of her two-and-six and then raped on her way home from the other side. Her Madam had been holding an enquiry into the mysterious disappearance of three rolls of toilet paper and she had missed her bus due to the length of the interrogation and her obvious inability to furnish an adequate answer as to whether toilet paper can grow legs and walk away by itself.

With the ongoing investigation in remission for the weekend, she had set off home, walking a dark, black four miles on foot. The thin Nguni maiden effortlessly balanced her parcel, a brown paper bag, on her head as she wended her way home. Her arms free, she occasionally clapped, her hands picking up the rhythm of the song she softly sang to herself; to imbue confidence but also to frighten away the *Tokolosh* imp who might be lurking in the wayside bushes.

Her Madam had laughed at her silly superstitions when she had put four bricks under the legs of her bed to elevate it, so the *Tokolosh,* who was very short, could never touch her face when she was asleep. But let Madam laugh, for was not serving from the left and clearing from the right the silliest of superstitions? Oh yes, let Madam laugh, for balanced on top of her head she had four, not three, rolls of toilet paper and a slowly defrosting frozen chicken she'd pinched from Madam's freezer.

It was not the *Tokolosh,* but the Devil in the form of Philomon Matwetwe, member of the TzotziBoys Gang, that dragged her under the dark bushes and had his way with her. Seven months later, after Madam had given Queeny

Bakateeny the sack for falling pregnant and chicken thievery (both crimes the result of allowing foxes into their respective hen houses), two things happened prematurely. One, she gave birth to a set of identical twins, both of them runts of the litter, and two, she died.

The poor preemies' survival could not be put down to the wonders of modern medicine but more to neglect, because all they ever received from Old Bakateeny, who had taken them in, was neglect. And even that was in small doses. But the runts, whose only fault was that they were infernal scoundrels, waxed with the seasons, and when they'd become young men, having finished their growth spurts, could best be described as 'stunted'.

It was these identical peas of a pod, whose only allure was the talk that the *Tokolosh* was their dad; these half pints, whose size was put down to the diminutive imp having sired them on the wayside that Friday evening long ago, who would be instrumental in bringing down the House of Tzotzi, which was now lead by Philomon Matwetwe, their real father.

Nobody was quite sure as to who was the older of the boys, so I'll introduce to you the one you don't know: "Ladies and Gentlemen ... the self-proclaimed contender to the crown of the Spider Weight Boxing Champion of the World ... weighing in at sixty kilos ... TapTap BeeSting Baa-kaaaa-teeeeeny!"

Yet in his prime, TapTap BeeSting Bakateeny had not abandoned the notion he still had a promising future as a boxer. No one had actually witnessed the legendary thirteen-punch combination he'd claimed to have developed. He would shadow box in an invisible whirlwind of fury which came to him so instinctively, or so he said, that he could not intentionally reproduce the flurry in slow motion, perchance anyone should desire to scientifically verify the combination's actual existence. People just had to take his word for it. Some were skeptical about the possibility that anybody, including TapTap BeeSting, could pepper blows so fast and furious he could land thirteen punches before his opponent could react.

I was among those doubters and I sought verification. Yours truly had the phantom thirteen-punch combination demonstrated by the only other person who'd claimed to have mastered such a lethal barrage of fisticuffs. That person was Duggy, my personal manservant. Moreover, besides being on a par with TapTap when fisticuffs were called for, he was also TapTap's twin brother. Duggy was a Bakateeny.

The demonstration had been good, in fact very good. Consider a punch so fast it cannot be seen – well maybe. Now consider the same with two punches that cannot be seen – enter the Twilight Zone. Three invisible punches? And the farmer took another load away. But thirteen?

WOW!

I was still not entirely convinced.

There are kaffirbooms, a type of shady tree, there are kaffir plums and kaffir lemons, both wonderful for making jams and marmalades. And there are kaffirtakkies, a form of footwear much favored by the well-shod African gentleman of fashion. They are a canvas sports shoe marketed as 'all stars/high tops', and that's what TapTap had bought to wear in his up-and-coming six-round bout against the Ferocious Fighter, SharpShoot Ali.

The kaffirtakkies were a matching red pair with thick white laces, whose particular purchase was financed through an advance from the bribe money. For a bunch of smackaroos, TapTap BeeSting was scheduled to take a dive in the second round.

Too much hype had been going around and its circulation had put the Township into a tizzy. The talk of the town was centered on TapTap's mystical combination which, all surmised, would raise him victorious. The TzotziBoys Gang controlled the betting and they had him favored to win at two-to-one. Half of Afrika was laying its bet on TapTap — betting on a sure thing. The Tzotzis, depending both on their strong-arm tactics and buying the Bee's sting, were taking the proceeds from these bets and re-betting them on SharpShoot Ali at nine-to-one, with Uncle BigBwana (You B Squared) from the City. A grand plan indeed: if TapTap took his dive in the second round as arranged, money was to be made.

But what if? What if dat li'le ol' TapTap got it into dat li'le ol' head of his to do something really stupid? What if he went overboard and won the match? Such an off-the-wall decision would leave the TzotziBoys Gang destitute, unable to pay off the bets that half of Afrika had laid on TapTap. It would rattle their whole power base and bring about their collapse and financial ruin. But if ifs and ands were pots and pans ... TapTap had yet to win the fight.

That was when the Bakateeny HardTimeBoys Gang sought me out for advice.

First on the agenda, I started cooking up curries. Next, wanting to keep my newfound stable of fighters happy, I gave the word to Duggy that he should pass on the good news to TapTap he could go out and buy another pair of red kaffirtakkies, if he was inclined, as everything was in order and under control.

Mental and psychological preparation for the fight was next on the agenda.

In an Afrika rampant with real spirits and rife with bogus erroneous notions, skeptical disregard of superstition does not diminish its coiled up potency in any way whatsoever. Be tolerant of what others believe and don't poke at idiosyncrasies. Scoff if you will, but when I recommended to TapTap that he should win the fight using magic, he eagerly and immediately adopted my suggestion. Duggy too; and well, why not? What, then, could be a more natural thing to accept for boys who half believed they were the sons of the *Tokolosh.* In Afrika, half belief is enough.

If during the fight, in moments of stress, I were to wrap my magic cloak around TapTap, a bumblebee, no less, would re-emerge from its folds, rejuvenated with a new verve. No opponent, no matter how vicious or malicious, would be able to withstand the revitalized barrage of blows, whose very vim was the fruit of a new found magical strength.

ALLAKAZZAM! was to be our magic word.

SharpShoot was a hard man to beat. I was adamant TapTap invest some time and energy in practice and preparation. I was not prepared to put my own life on the line solely on the off chance that there was indeed something; both to that thirteen-punch combination and to the power of positive suggestion.

The reason, explained to me by Duggy and Co, that the thirteen-punch combination had yet to make its public debut was because it (the combination) was essentially a lethal counter attack and TapTap had to wait for an opening before he could implement it. Unfortunately, since up till now no such opening had presented itself, I was adamant that lack of training would not be our downfall. They turned out every day, TapTap, the contender and Duggy, his jousting partner, perhaps both to humor me and also to share in the pure delight of sparring against each other.

It was enchanting to witness the speed of those two ebony-hard bodies of bone and tendon, yet lithe and supple as mambas, twining and intertwining in a jittering dance of dodges and head-ducks. The flurry of punches and blows and attacks and counter attacks was so fast and furious the eye was bewildered.

These bursts of expended pugilistic energy could not be kept up for any great length of time, so we took many breaks to practice and discuss our fight strategy. Lord

Queensbury, the founder of modern boxing, sat up in his grave while TapTap and Duggy showed *their* appreciation of our plan by vigorously enacting victory dances with their tongues gleefully protruding through the gaps in their respective front teeth.

On the morning of the fight, Afrika awoke to the buzz and squawk of short wave radios as, across the continent, antennas were strung up to catch the signal. From baobab to baobab, from dried out acacias to camels' necks, the copper strands were strung as people began tuning in, searching for the station. At 4:30pm sharp, Radio Bantu was to begin its transmission – 770 MgHz on the short wave dial. Live from the only school's only soccer field in the Township of New Bright-Tin to the rest of Afrika.

Afrika was holding its breath. If the radio-listening audience could not see it, at least they would be able to visualize and feel the overly expected and much anticipated thirteen-punch combination. Later that day, when Afrika would have resumed breathing properly, I was hoping, barring any unmanageable crises, to be counted in amongst them.

But the best-laid plans of mice and men ... Crisis number one – the spotlights were on the blink.

The promoters gave explanation that the malfunction was due to the spotlights' copper wiring being multi-disciplinable. The copper had been appropriated by *other parties* and was now being resold as antenna wire. This meant the fight would have to take place during the day and everybody knows, be he young or old, cretin or politician, that magic works better under the folds of darkness.

A. A. Milne had Pooh Bear warn us, more than once: 'you never can tell with bees'. As forewarned is forearmed, I thank you, so very much, Mr Milne. *Hapote'ah pe l'satan* (he who opens his mouth for Satan).

And so Mr Pooh Bear, as sure as beans is beans, right

there and then, literally as near to the ring of the bell for round number one as can be nightmarishly possible, popped up ... Crisis number two – the unfortunate case of a certain autonomous thinker of a bee. A bee who nearly blew it all.

I acknowledge and accept that physiological parameters had kept TapTap BeeSting's brain to the minimum size it was. But how can any brain, as petite as it may be, be so comprehensively, so totally and effectively blank, it would leave me wondering if I had actually succeeded in penetrating it in the first place?

The answer to the question, as to whether he had any notion whatsoever about what we'd been scheming and conniving the last couple of weeks, sent a chill up my spine which blossomed out into a shudder which came to rest in the center of my bowels. Luckily, as we were in the boys' toilets, I had a place to which I could retire. To a doorless cubicle I scurried, where I could ponder and contemplate the ups of our confident past and the downs of our immediate pessimistic future. In peace, insulated from all outside interferences by an all-enveloping cloud of curried vapor, I put things into perspective and searched out a solution.

While Afrika had been bartering for batteries to get its transistors cranked-up and running, I had been busy taking care of all last minute measures. I had organized my mental list of jobs and worked through them methodically. It would not do to slip up due to negligence.

As I was to be going in as Dr Mandrake N Shareef, cut doctor and devout Indian Mohammedan, I knew if I threw out enough *hamduallahs* and *insha'Allah*s, my magic word, ALLAKAZZAM, would not sound out of place. The 'N' in my name stood for Naaidoo.

For my footwear I had selected, as a political statement, my ventilated, two-tone black and whites. I had seen to the pointy silver toecaps, shining them with Silvo, after which Duggy, my valet, buffed up the black lower half of the shoes with black spit and Shade of Night – Leather and Shoe Polish. The upper section was whitened with black spit and Full Moon – Leather and Shoe Polish. A light wipe of Vaseline enhanced their separately developed sheen.

My black and white checkered trousers were pressed under a hot iron and a damp rag, tempering their knife-edge creases. The garment was intentionally cut high in the hip and short in the leg, leaving exposed for all to admire, a pleasing to the eye fashion statement – my white socks, ornamented with a myriad of black paisleys. Sharp!

I made a mental note, reminding myself to ask my friends if their valets took care of any minor mending of clothes; the sewing on of missing buttons for instance.

It was agony to watch as Duggy worked on my trousers like he was sewing buttons on a brick wall with a rubber needle. And why, oh why, did he have to use red thread when he replaced my white shirt buttons with black ones? Why?

My favorite cotton button-up shirt, which suffered from brilliant bleach radiation, with extra long cuffs and pointy collar, was now bleeding to death through its buttonholes.

Duggy's mercurial behavior sometimes knobbles our relationship.

No jacket.

For headgear, Duggy had laid out the black cap with white polka-stars. I reviewed myself in the mirror with it perched on my head. To whichever angle I tilted, it still made me look ridiculous. Stars always clashed with paisleys. I was to be from top-to-toe, so I discarded it and dyed my hair black, using a couple of dabs of Shade of Night – Leather and Shoe Polish. Sweeping my locks back, I plastered them into place with a smear of Vaseline: the wet crow look. I would make a final run through with a comb later. I hoped it would hold its sheen as it dried.

I had trimmed my Fidel Castro down to a Sheik Obed and, to complete the Sol Zinitzin look, shaved my moustache down to stubble. I dusted what was left of my beard with kohl I had on hand for darkening around the eyes. And a smidgen of Vaseline to complete the effect. I looked ten years younger. I had toyed with the idea of leaving my beard its natural white, but that would have hinted at some gross syndrome and I wanted to look as normal as possible.

To top it all, my magic cape; a full-length wrap-around cloak, black on the outside, and its reverse side lined with magenta sateen, breaking my colour statement together with its guidelines. But in the Township, very few men would be wearing matching outfits. It would help me blend in.

We left for the fight in a borrowed car. We were going to meet up with TapTap at the venue. Duggy drove, as he knew the way. You have to be born and bred in the briar patch to know your way in and to know your way out. The campaign against the House of Tzotzi was gaining momentum. Inside my traditional looking doctor's bag, neatly packed away, together with cotton balls, Vaseline and Mercurochrome, our regimented battalions lay waiting with lined up companies of orchestrated guile, cunning, magic and superstition, all anticipating action.

We made our way across the hot, sun-baked earth, across the soccer field in the direction of the boys' toilets, making a detour around the still vacant boxing ring, its podium trapping wind-blown newspapers and plastic bags along its base. Nobody was about yet, except for the guard, who was taking advantage of the shade under the judges' wooden table. He was fast asleep and the plastic bag which had swirled in with a gust and landed flapping on his face did not seem to disturb him in the least. Except for the buzzing flies, all Afrika was gathering its strength for the big event.

The girls' toilets, a separate building next to ours, was booked for the opposition. They were already ahead on points; the smell in their ablution block was only a little less bracing than in ours, but nevertheless an unfair advantage. We, on the other hand, struggled to complete our deep breathing relaxation routine – in through the nose and out through the mouth – while waiting for TapTap. But I suppose one can eventually get used to the nature of all manner of things.

Enter the bearer of crisis number two. It was TapTap, who had *it* stuffed in the bottom of his kitbag alongside his new red kaffirtakkies with white laces. He extracted *it* – a second pair, with white laces; only these takkies were blue.

I was already in character so you will have to imagine a Hindustananian accent to appreciate the essence of my superlatives: "What the dickens Man? What in the name of all things holy are you trying to prove? Fires of damnation Man, what colour *takkies* are you going to wear now? Only the greatness of *Allah* can pull us through this one." It was then that I had retired to the loo.

Moving matter, *hamduallah*, solved the problem at both ends.

"*Insha'Allah*. I have the solution," I announced through the fog. "One and one it is!"

TapTap: "Two?"

Duggy: "Hey! I knew that."

"Doubly wrong – you dastard imbeciles. It's one blue *takkie* and one red one. TapTap, young fellow, you must wear odd shoes!"

Very-Sharp.

I was still indisposed, so I could only visualize the duo, enamored with the solution, wasting their energy in vigorously reenacting victory dances, with both their tongues gleefully protruding through the gaps in their front teeth. It's a tough world.

We gloved up and huddled together for final instructions. I found unbearable the effort of squinting to make totally sure I had simultaneously established eye contact with both of them, so I addressed each one separately:

"TapTap, young fellow, remember what we discussed about conserving energy during the fight. The black blood of Shaka the Zulu runs through your veins and it will give you heart. The spirit of Tokolosh, your father, will give you strength. Fight well my very good friend."

And to Duggy: "It is time. I hope this will not be our last goodbye."

I led TapTap out. The crowd parted to let us through. FlatNose, the announcer, togged out in spotless white, his black hands and head contrasting sharply with his outfit, had just finished introducing the Ferocious Fighter, SharpShoot Ali, to the masses. The white heat had baked up a quivering mirage over the ring and the announcer's head and hands seemed to float ethereally, reminiscent of a black art show. Extra-Sharp.

As we approached the ring, FlatNose's earthly body emerged from the mirage's ripples, re-attaching itself to its black extremities. It was a hot afternoon and the high temperature would siphon off the fighters' strength from round one.

The heat was already starting to take its toll and I clambered up into the ring with a grunt. The changes in diet I'd been enjoying seemed to have added a thickness to my torso. But soon, when this was all over, I would shed the responsibility of carrying around a sixty-kilogram fighter and lose some weight.

"... And the contender for the thirteen-punch combination and for his first knock-out, in the blue and red shoes ..." TapTap did a showy shuffle with his blue-and-reds and the crowd went wild. "… BeeSting, TapTap Baaakaaa …" The rest was lost as the crowd took up a chant.

"Thirteen! Thirteen!"

"… And the referee this afternoon, who is registered with SABO, an avid supporter of boxing, who is also our own Beloved Deputy-Inspector of Bantu affairs … Inspector Martinus van der Merwe." The crowd murmured their approval, endorsing the choice of a neutral outsider as an impartial referee. He was probably the only white man who would have dared to enter the Township alone.

FlatNose raised his hands for silence so they could begin singing the national anthem. The harmony of thousands, each voice knowing instinctively what was required as they took up the refrain of *Nkosi Sikelel'i Afrika*, undulated across Afrika when the radio-listening audience joined in. Each and every one of them intuitively synchronized, knowing when to come in and when to recede. It ended. Afrika had vibrated in singular harmony. Simba-Afrika had roared.

Inspector Martinus van der Merwe, assuming his role as referee, climbed into the center of the ring. Although a dyed-in-the-wool pragmatist, he could never get over the singing. He was always asking himself and his driver, Bantu Constable Ndlovo, why the blacks could never get together and hold a couple of rehearsals in order to co-ordinate harmonies and show some civilized respect for their anthem? He never got a direct answer and, running out of patience, his aborted quest for knowledge generally spawned a reprimand when his irritation closed the subject by telling Bantu Constable Ndlovo he was a "Cheeky Kaffir" and to "Stop staring at me as if I was mad."

He motioned both sides to gather round for instructions.

"Hey listen! As far as I'm concerned you're just a bunch of cheeky Kaffirs. But you both know the rules; so don't try any hotshot moves with me. One of you is stronger than the other one and the other one is faster than the first one, so it's a fair fight. Don't disappoint the crowd or make a fool out of me, because if either one of you has bleddy brought me all the way down here for bleddy nothing, I'll do more then bleddy call him a 'Bleddy Cheeky You-Know-What'. I want a good show – you both understand? Six rounds is a long fight in this hellhole. Use your brains, if you have any. Don't take water between rounds and conserve your strength for the end. On the sound of the bell, come out fighting and may the best one of you win."

No one can do better justice when it comes to describing a fight than Nigel QuickLips, Bantu Radio's sports commentator and man on the spot. But even he was at a loss for words. All he could manage was a gasped "*Tyhini Thixo* – Oh my God!" before the roar of the crowd made broadcasting impractical. The radio-listening audience had to pensively wait for the end of the round before the crowd quieted down enough for Nigel QuickLips to get a word in edgeways.

"Leddies und gentulmun of the radio-listening udience. It seems thut the mun in the red und blue shoes hus gone mud. Eeayeees. He is a whirlwind of punches und the queshtion we're ull usking ourselves is, is this going to be TupTup's strutugy in the next round und ull the way intoo the rest of the fight?

"ShupShoot hus not retuliated with even one blow, but he is cuvering up very well indeed. TupTup hus defunuteley won this round on points but I don't think he hus done much to punish his upponunt ..."

In his corner, TapTap sat on the stool taking deep breaths, refueling his lungs with oxygen sucked from the hot air. There was nothing much for me to do except wipe the sweat off his face, remind him about what we had discussed about conserving energy, and take the wise King Solomon's advice – hope for the best.

King Solomon counsels in Ecclesiastes that we should 'give a portion to seven and also to eight.' A wise Rabbi had taught me that seven is a number we can bank on, a measurable entity, whose archetype is in the seven days of creation. Eight, on the other hand, represents what we see as the uncontrolled influences that juggle with our fate. I had cast my bread upon the waters and, knowing who my customers were, could only hope for the best.

Rounds two and three were shades of round one, as TapTap flailed away. Nigel QuickLips did not relay them to Afrika as the transmission was taking a commercial break.

(*i Stohney GingaBeer*)

Then he was back on the air. "Eeayeees. Und walcome buck to our broadcust. We are in the break afta round three und you have all missed un extra-vagunza of boxing. TupTup is defunuteley winning on points as ShupShoot hus yet to lund a punch. We are all waiting in unticipashun for the thirteen-punch combinashun, but I cun tell you TupTup hus been laying it on a bit thick. Honusteley I don't think he cun keep up the pace. He is loosing tooo much leequwid und is already showing signs of exhauschun.

"I don't believe it, peopul, but something extremuley unorthodox is huppening. I don't believe there is a precidunt for this in ull uf boxing history, but the refaree hus gone over to TupTup's corna und is kicking him in the buttocks. I do believe he is pointing at TupTup's empty watta bottle und culling him a 'Bleddy stupid Kaffir!' ShapShoot's corna are up in ums. They are claiming unfair motivashun on the part of the referee ..."

At the sound of the bell for round four the crowd began to chant with Afrika picking up on their lead – "Thirteen! Thirteen! Thirteen!" The devotees knew it was now or never. But the Thirteen Fan Club fizzled out towards the end of the round when the played-out TapTap, who could hardly keep his hands in the air to defend himself, spent the last minute running desperately, trying to stay out of SharpShoot's reach. He was saved by the bell and he teetered to our corner depleted, his body shivering with muscular exhaustion. SharpShoot's corner saw him taking water again and knew they were going to nail TapTap in the next round.

"Well done TapTap, a grand performance indeed, but now it's time to rope in the black arts." So saying, I wrapped my magic cloak around his pathetically trembling body with an "*ALLAKAZZAM!*" Would the magic save us as the bell rang for round number five? Would they, the crowd, notice that a new revitalized man would emerge from under my cape and would they pick up on it, catch on that we had used magic?

SharpShoot shot out of his corner with instructions from his manager to finish the whole thing off once and for all. His opponent, his red and blues unsteadily planted on the canvas, quavered, as SharpShoot Ali with cocky expertise, lined him up for the coup-de-grâce. The crowd grew silent as they watched SharpShoot, rather unsportingly, wind himself up for a final right hook to the defenseless chin. The uneasy hush spread and the whole of Afrika winced as a poised SharpShoot let loose.

But the blow never landed, it dissipated when our man, in his switched around red and blue kaffirtakkies, magically found inexplicable strength and rose like a surprise Phoenix from the ashes of defeat and counter-attacked. Nobody actually witnessed anything, including SharpShoot, who, thinking he had been struck by lightning, keeled over and fell flat on his face – out for the count. But Afrika felt it ... and knew it. For the skeptics, Nigel QuickLips' "Hauw!" said it all. The mother of all counter-attacks, the thirteen-punch combination, had been born.

The referee, Inspector Van der Merwe, believing SharpShoot to be a silly victim of heat exhaustion, didn't even bother to count him out, but chose rather to leave the ring in disgust. But not before he gave the downed man a departing kick in the ribs to make entirely sure that he had no more fight left in him.

My only fear had been that the crowd would notice that TapTap, who had started the fight with a red shoe on his right foot and a blue on his left, had magically ended it with a red shoe on the left and a blue on the right.

Even taking into account potential disaster over the odd coloured kaffirtakkies, we had all acquitted ourselves admirably under the circumstances; but it was time to take our leave. This time, when the crowd parted, it was Duggy I was leading and TapTap who was riding piggyback, hidden by the folds of my cape.

The old? The old switcheroo, of course.

Food for thought, indeed. Even with my powers, this was one book I'd have to start reading from the beginning. I was happy that I'd made a security check before I'd tucked myself in. I flicked off the bedside lamp and made myself comfy with my four favorite pillows. Chiropractor's orders: I sleep on my side with two pillows under my head, one between my knees and the fourth one to snuggle up to in lieu of wife and to provide support for my free arm.

That night I dreamt I was suckling from a black teat on a white she-hyena. My dream twin brother Freddy was attached to the other breast.

# CHAPTER THREE

I awoke with a start, jumped out of bed and headed for my en-suite 'ablution block', a new word I'd learnt. Nothing happened. Last night's delicacies, which the Master had probably independently tithed from the taxman, were not showing any charity this morning. With pajama pants around my ankles, I shuffled to the bedroom to retrieve the manuscript. And back again, where I plonked myself down back on the bowl for another attempt. Reading on the toilet, though no doubt a proctological hazard, was one way to help time take its course. I began at the beginning.

**If Truth be Told: The Memoirs of Quentin Locke**
***In the beginning ...***

To gratify my craving as a sentimental parent and because we have a deep seated longing to have our children pilgrim to the land of our birth, I visited, with my son, the birthplace of his ancestors. After enjoying the advantages of modern air travel, we found ourselves before a dilapidated edifice whose crumbling walls were ample testimony to a generation already passed. I pointed it out reverently to my son the house I was born in. Down the hill and around the bend, adjacent to the prison, lay the cemetery I hallowed as the burial place of my parents.

Everything had changed so mercilessly that even fond remembrance could not help me recognize the old familiar haunts. After wandering around for a day or two, speculating about a past that had left so little outward trace, we departed. I noted, even though nothing can have a more momentous influence on the lives of our children than an intimate knowledge of their fathers and grandfathers, it couldn't be supplied by a fleeting visit to their graves.

On the eve of my departure I browsed through the spine-cracked library in my father's study, hoping to find a literary companion to accompany me on my journey home. Not wanting to re-digest the tomes of my youth, my hope was to find something I'd not yet read. The sentimentality of the moment directed my eyes to a book entitled *Letters of a Jewish Father to his Son* – how appropriate for the occasion. Even more appropriately, when I randomly flipped it open, the paragraph that engaged my attention was as if in anticipation of my earlier musings on the fleeting respect for tradition.

It was from Chapter Six, a chapter concerning the Grandfather of modern Jewish literature, Mendli Mocher Sfarim:

*If the children would know anything of the past they must turn to our literature where the artists of our race have immortalized in pictures which portray it in all of its entirety and in all its beauty ... had a deluge engulfed the world and submerged the Jewish town in 19C Russia, the investigator would have reconstructed and repopulated them without omitting any details, if by some chance Mendeli's writings had been saved.*

The advantages of modern air travel aside, and without being so presumptuous as to even imagine I could come close to emulating MMS, or even contributing to Jewish literature, it occurred to me I could save other Fathers from the 'home town Hajj' by putting down in writing the experiences of my generation. Why myself for this undertaking? Having been blessed with a cinemagraphic memory of infallible proportions and with nothing to utilize my time for the duration of my flight, it would be a fine opportunity to get some chapters cut and dried before landing. The only drawback to my sentimentality was finding myself in the unenviable position of being an honorable person to whom even the contemplation of an untruth would be intolerable.

Being so restricted, as in not being able to resort to imaginative soarings of fantasy, I felt the results might be of a staid and boring nature, holding no attraction to the reader. So with a nothing-ventured-nothing-gained burst of optimism, we begin with some background before we loop the loop into chapter one — fasten your seatbelts, folks!

## Background

This is no vague account of the product of time but rather what will soon be called history:

By convention our family is the Prima Family of Upholders. We tend to do things in our own traditional way. In our family, when tradition is mentioned, we aren't referring to something of a generic, *Fiddler on the Roof* variety.

My father is fluent in four languages, but this does not help him get dressed in the morning so he can go off for his rendezvous with Costas at the café on the corner to play pinball.

My father was, and still is, a renowned Pinball Wizard. His wizardry remains unchallenged. He can push a machine a tremor away from a tilt and laugh in its numerical box-face as free games clack onto the board. He turned his hobby into a career and, at the age of eighty-plus, still has an uncanny control of that metal ball. His skill is beyond the natural coordination of eye and hand, and Costas insists that my father telekinetically controls the ball, his thoughts sending it around under the glass, zigzagging at unnatural angles that do not hold with the basic law of nature and physics, namely the angle of incidence should equal the angle of reflection. Indeed, Costas has a lot of theories.

Costas, a Cypriot expatriate, the retired proprietor of The Oasis Snacks Café, used to own a couple of pinball machines in the old days, which turned him into a sort of living Greek demigod.

He contends that my father, when he's cheesed off with something, can make the pinball ball jump up and crack the glass top. Indeed, Costas says a lot of things, but pinging the plate glass top of a machine from the underside with enough power in that steel orb to cause the glass to crack is no mean feat. It is beyond the scope of even the above average player, not to mention normal sane men. His claim though, that Father has some weird facilities, is not groundless.

In our family when we mention facilities we don't mean cloakrooms.

Except for pinball, Costas and my father have nothing in common, and yet he is also my father's best friend. They used to play snooker until my father's fifth lumber vertebrae jumped out of place and played havoc with his sciatic nerve. Costas, who generally lost these snooker tournaments (he was convinced that my father won only because he cheated by using his telekinetic powers), once suggested Father use his paranormal facilities less on the coloured balls and more on realigning his wonky vertebrae. Crack! Bang went another plate glass pinball cover along with Costa's sage advice.

My father's big brother was my Uncle Bert. Father's summation of Uncle Bert was *groyse Petrus Oysgevaksen* (an oaf of a man). Father, who speaks a fluent Lithuanian Yiddish and has a poetic bent as well as being quite literate, is always being called upon to read and translate letters from the old country. The bottom line being:

*Rahmonus* – mercy – please send some money to your impoverished *landsman*. Landsman, someone who shares your place of birth, was the first Yiddish word I picked up. 'Yok' (Gentile – derogatory) and 'Peruvnick' (acronym for members of the Polish and Russian Union – a socialist aid society for down and out immigrants – a bum), subsequent enrichments to my vocabulary, I was told to drop.

His standard warning before parting ways, I for school and he for *work*, was usually: "Stick by your landsman, watch out for the Yoks and don't ever be a Peruvnick ... and I can't help you with your homework today because I'm out playing pinball." This was usually said while squeezing the flesh under my chin between his thumb and second knuckle of his first finger in order to make sure he had my utmost attention. For your enlightenment: a landsman can never be a Yok and the opposite holds, a Yok can never be a landsman, but both of them can be Peruvnickim – the worst of the worst. If this boggle is not a foil for your erudition, you obviously do not speak fluent Lithuanian Yiddish with a poetic bent.

Tradition dictates that the Upholder title is to be passed on from generation to generation and to only one candidate. My paternal grandfather was an Upholder. I never appreciated him personally, but his antics were legendary. His intentional poaching to death of a cook in a mineworkers' kitchen by tipping over a boiling cauldron of soup has already become Upholder Lore. Granddad, stepping into the breach, had doctored up the consommé, turning it into a satisfyingly thick gruel. Apparently the cook, as the late night story goes, had too many hands in too many pots, leaving hungry miners' stomachs grumbling in the wake of his greed.

My father is not an Upholder. His big brother, my Uncle Bert, was. He, Uncle Bert, proved himself a versatile holder of this singular title when he killed a Yok while in the army during the war (the Yok was on his side, not the enemy's).

In his infantry battalion, where men were giants, Uncle Bert was a mountain. He was also the battalion Physical Training Instructor; basically the most feared ecological system our universe can sustain. Mighty soldiers of valor and veterans of bloody campaigns trembled to attention when he made his entrance. His all-time favorite – beyond his speciality; unarmed combat, and his hobby; bodily harm – was the close combat course, which included advanced instruction on how to stick one's bayonet into the enemy's guts and then trigger off a round into the popped belly. The rifle's recoil aided in extracting the bayonet. (Costas: "For every action there is an equal and opposite reaction.") The bullet, of course, finished the job. But that's not how Uncle Bert did it.

'Give me a lever long enough and a fulcrum to rest it on and I will move the earth.' This, besides being another of Costas' theories, was Uncle Bert's modus operandi (he was also a lover of physics). And it turned out that besides attaining mythical demigodship, Costas was also something of an ancient Greek mathematician/physicist.

The barracks where Uncle Bert was stationed during the war had a large, oblong storeroom with a long metal locker dividing it. Piles of wrestling mats used for unarmed combat training and sneaking midmorning naps took up the backside space behind the locker. Some of the piles were nearly as high as the locker itself – about eight feet. The compartmentalized locker was chock-a-block with equipment. It weighed a ton.

A lesson in simplicity: Uncle Bert, who was resting on a pile of those mats, adjusted his Atlasian shoulders, anchoring them snuggly against the top edge of the locker. With bent knees, the soles of his brown army boots firmly braced against the wall, he tensed his cordian thigh muscles (the strongest muscle in the human anatomy) and, summoning up his deep inner strength, pushed. That did it – instant gratification. The cabinet tippled over onto the Yok who was fiddling with some ammunition prior to it being stored away in locker number six. Uncle Bert didn't stick around to squeegee up the mess. He was always decidedly ratty when disturbed during his regular midmorning naps.

According to Costas, Uncle Bert tended to get too involved. He claimed the steam-rollering would have been better accomplished by tippling the locker, arse over kettle, using telekinetic powers. But Uncle Bert's passion for physics had won the day. He summed up the whole exercise for Costas: the lever was the eight-foot high locker and the wall of the storeroom acted as the fulcrum. A lovely case of applied physics.

Costas: "You see, kids; physics can be fun."

Again according to Costas, the reason my father never attained Upholdership, though his facilities made him more than an adequate candidate, was because he married my mother. She ruled our suburb as the Great White Elephant Queen of Brakston Park (GWEQ of BP). She regarded work as the natural state of man and she lorded over her subjects, with whom she had nothing in common. She belonged to the People of Zion and they belonged to the Church of Zion. They celebrated New Year in December. She did not. They celebrated Easter and Pentecost traveling the country in buses, bursting with good will and B.O. Their destination days away to join other congregants in hymn harmonizing to the Good Lord. She never rode on buses and she used Mum for Men roll-on.

My father classified her subjects Heathens and claimed they stank of marijuana – *dagga* he called it. It was only out of head over heels love and consideration for her and her royal standing that he abdicated his position to Uncle Bert. To this day he insists he was duped and she was to blame that he never attained his full potential in life. The truth of the matter was, and still is, that she totally forbade it – and that was that. Or as they say in Yiddish: 'Datch dat'.

Yes, we did live in the South, and the Jews who hailed from other places, considered us white trash. They had us well targeted. Even the Jews from the upgrade suburbs of our town, who resided in Bluestrand (sometimes black with tar white beaches, rolling surf, surfboards, speedos and Coppertone Tan Don't Burn suntans), or River Drive Park (gigantic trees shading green lawns from the hot, summer sun and a garden boy, who is really a man, straining the leafy debris from the pool), would have nothing to do with us Jews from Brakston Park (yellowish dried grass with an ecosystem of grasshoppers and stick insects kept under control by five or six continually pecking-for-survival hens, and one rooster who wakes everyone within a five hundred miles radius or more, with his mighty crowing. Early every a.m., with chronometer-like precision, he starts a chain reaction. Neighborhood after neighborhood, in ever out-spreading ripples of converse waves, is crowed awake by sleepy cocks echoing Rooster's first light alarum). And because Brakston Park was up on top of the hill, you didn't have to be intellectually blessed to appreciate the inevitability that fate had us marked – we were indelibly stamped Hillbillies.

The long and the short and the tall of it is, besides my mother being the Great White Elephant Queen of Brakston Park (which in all probability made me the defacto Great White Buffalo Prince of Brakston Park), I happened to *be*, only because my mother strictly forbade it, the next generation's Upholder.

## A Knight of Afrika
### *Duggy comes to the rescue*

"Good Morning Sub A Class." I was nearly six and the first day of my schooling began with the whole class standing at attention, practicing to parrot back in complete sing song unison: "Good morning Mrs McGregor," for the umpteenth time. The day ended, in much the same vein, with everybody going through the same rigmarole, except this time, influenced by the good graces of the God Chronos, who unlike his own children whom he'd swallowed, us he regurgitated back into the outside world when the rendition was amended to a 'Good afternoon Sub A class,' and a, 'Good afternoon Mrs McGregor.' Like new recruits we were being mercilessly drilled in school decorum.

The motto of the school, the Jabotinsky Hebrew Day School, was *Hamila Haivrit Go'elet*, which when translated informs us: The Hebrew Word Redeems. I'm still waiting. I was in the Sub A class, an abbreviation for Substandard A – which was about the level of education I was to receive there.

A Day School is so called because the attending pupils don't stay overnight. We went home when the school day was over but were required to bring our own lunches – generally Marmite sandwiches – to provide us with sufficient kilojoules to burn as we exerted ourselves through a longer than normal schedule of classes. In addition to the regulation government-supplied curriculum, we had to learn Hebrew, which explained the inexorable extension to our boredom.

Afternoon brought its relief, together with my extra-curricular activities. It was then that I went to Upholders School in order to accommodate the country's education laws, which conscripted every able-bodied boy or girl until the age of sixteen or until they passed their J.C. Junior Certificate of Education – a Yok's milestone in life.

Except for the occasional re-toning-up session, my Sub A class moved from the "Good morning; Good afternoon Mrs McGregor" mode to learning the skills of writing, reading and conversing in three languages.

English Reader: this is Janet, this is John.

Hebrew Reader: Gad – Gad yeled gadol (Gad – Gad is a big boy).

Afrikaans Reader: Boggem sê die aap (The monkey grunts).

And then I had my first shocking realization: I discovered with a thud that I was a tad more than mildly dyslectic. Aside from Hebrew starting from the wrong side of the page, I encountered b's that kept on getting confused with d's. Teetering on the straight and narrow and simultaneously minding my p's and q's was a paramount effort which generally ended in dismal failure. This particular little train was going to have a tough time just staying on the tracks.

My second realization was both shocking and remarkable. The institute I had been enrolled in was not a school at all, but a fantastically realistic reincarnation of Stalag 61, a German POW camp made famous by Hollywood. This was no film set though, but a life-like replica constructed on a 1:1 scale. A pre-virtual reality hell. The teachers playing the part of the Jerry Goons, and Fat Rat the headmaster was none other than the Obershmoobercommandant himself. With us on *appel,* three times a day – before school and after both first and second breaks, in lines, stragglers rounded up and accounted for and frogmarched into class – escape was impossible.

Mr Smith, the maths master, who had surrendered at Tobruk and was a bona fide ex-POW, must have viewed the whole fuss and palaver as another bad case of *déjà-vu*. Poor bastard.

The prognosis for the next decade or so seemed

decidedly bleak. After raising the point with my extra-curriculum mentors, it was unanimously decided – a decision I had no part in but was happy to adopt – that I would crib my homework, cheat in my tests and take advantage of every opportunity to get away with doing as little as possible. This strategy was intended to provide me with more time for my extra-mural apprenticeship.

In our family when we talk about extra-mural activities we don't mean spending the afternoon sharing the cricket outfield with a herd of grasshoppers as the least important player of the under-13 B team. The school had some excellent players in its various teams but I had decided not to join them in their gladiatorial glory. Inter-school cricket matches were spent alternatively practicing and improving my skills as a grasshopper stalker or trying to bond with them in the outfield.

Once, when fielding in the deep covers, I was drawn out of my study of brown grasshoppers when someone yelled in my direction. "Catch it!" Instinctively I dove full length, my arm outstretched, with cupped hand extended in anticipation. An adrenal glow surged through my body. I had actually succeeded in catching it. The next yelled command; "Throw it back man!" went against the grain. It was not something I immediately wanted to do, but the rules of the game are the rules of the game and that's how we play. So the poor grasshopper was hurled with all my strength towards the center of the cricket pitch. It arched out for all of six feet before it landed, righted itself, and hopped away to freedom.

I can fully understand the next bit of verbal abuse launched in my direction: "Wake up you idiot!" Take it from their point of view; watching a boy dive across the grass, pretending to catch a ball and, after examining his phantom catch intently for a couple of seconds, hurl it back in their direction. They must have thought I was mad.

Occasionally, and only occasionally, a loophole is found

in the cricket rulebook, which allows me to go in to bat. Now the dilemma is all mine. Should I tonk the ball for a six or should I let myself be bowled out for a no score duck? Invariably my better judgment ruled and I would decide on a quick dismissal. Keeping a low profile was the recommended requirement for an apprentice Upholder.

But when all is said and done, I'm sure you're aching to know how I cheated in my exams and are probably mulling over as to whether, if this would be the only thing garnered from this tale, it would be reading time well invested. I'm sorry to be a big disappointment, but I must implement Reid's Boredom Theory: The less told the better.

Patrick Reid, in his epic book, The Colditz Story, cameos the life style (Goon baiting sounded like fun) and the escape attempts of allied prisoners of war captured and interned in Colditz Castle, a facility for the most incorrigible of war prisoners, most of them veterans of disregarding the Escape-is-Impossible theory. Escaping from POW camps has been described as the most exciting sport a man could play at. The Geneva Convention was used as a rulebook. After unsuccessful escape attempts the truants were recaptured with a "Hände hoche!" and sent off to the cooler, a prison within a prison. Our Stalag also had a cooler – we called it detention.

Reid also admits in his book that he does not tell it all, claiming that it would be a disservice to the next generation of POWs if all were divulged. He proposes that with many hours of boredom on hand, the POW of the future will reinvent and rediscover how to shore up tunnels or construct secret hideaways and hatchways out of bed boards. I'm a firm believer in his theory because personal experience has shown me that it works. Accordingly, the only cheating technique I'm going to share with you was one that fused together while I was redundantly positioned in the outfield of the cricket pitch, doing exactly nothing. Reid's boredom and the grasshoppers set the mind in motion, together, of course, with a catalyst from Costas.

Costas has some theories regarding enemy annihilation: strategically, always attack the enemy's weakest point and tactically, always target the weakest link. I don't know how original these theories are and how they would actually work in practice, but nevertheless I decided to give rein to my instincts while leaving all compromising assessments for later. I was going all out.

As the proposed escapade would probably require me to cross the line of the law, I had to get my tutors' permission. With this in mind I put my theories before them. The grasshoppers had led me to the Stalag's weakest link – Douglas.

Douglas was a talented man. He was all of janitor, night watchman and groundsman. His front-toothless grin was the nicest reception I ever received from anyone at the Stalag. His peaked leatherette cap, generally pushed up at a cocky angle, signaled to all and sundry his happy demeanor.

It was one of his jobs to mark out the boundary lines on the outfield with white paint. The technique began by laying the long hosepipe along the intended line. Then using the hosepipe as his guide, he would splash the paint along the pipe with a block brush and a short, sharp snapping wrist motion, creating on its removal a perfectly straight goal line, halfway line, or whatever line. The paintbrush had to be held about six inches above the grass for best results. The job was accomplished with much bending. His arms simply weren't long enough to reach the required paint application height without creating havoc to his lower back.

In his capacity as groundsman he was charged with maintaining the many superfluous playing fields, both surrounding and laying siege to the barracks. It was also his responsibility to scare off the besieger's army of grasshoppers who had us blockaded. Twice a week, up and down and down and up, then backwards and forwards he valiantly fought off the enemy with his lawnmower. Marching along in straight lines, bent over the mower's handles and with his head held high, he gallantly fought off the invaders, with the grasshoppers skittering away from the revolving blades. This battle heralded his lower back's death knell.

It was not only this bravery that drew me to him; Douglas was also Stalag's weak link. He was my target. For my plan to work, I had to enter into a friendship with Duggy.

Duggy lived in a room behind the boys' toilets. I could tell it was never intended for human habitation because the door didn't reach the floor. It was shy by some four inches; maybe to compensate for the windowless walls. It was basically a storeroom with a bed. This was Duggy's happy home, into which I was soon invited as his welcomed guest.

I had ingratiated myself to him by showing keen interest in his theory that the extraction of his front teeth improved his sex life (Costas told me I should work this one out for myself — strangely enough, for once he seemed at a loss for an explanation), and also by providing a sympathetic ear and sage counsel on how to repair the damage done to his back. Father's fifth lumber vertebra had, by association, made me an expert on the subject. Duggy was also very happy to accept, beyond my sympathy and advice, father's leftover medicines.

The friendship developed into a bond of brotherhood when I presented him with a worn-out bar-mitzvah blazer. I dropped by every day, either at first or second break, ostensibly to hide from the Goons as I lit up a cigarette, and to share my Marmite sandwiches with him. He would always join me in a smoke. He used Best Blend tobacco, which he rolled in brown paper torn from covers of expired exercise books. This paper was easier on his lungs than a rectangular piece of brown shopping bag paper crumpled to make it more combustible. Occasionally I would offer Duggy one of mine to give him a taste of what could be in store for him – the high life.

And then the day came when Duggy slipped up. He let on to something that made everything so much easier. On a second break once, he accepted one of mine but carried on rolling one of his BBs. "This is for after when I chase the grasshopper," he told me. The *one* of his soon became *two* of his and the finished products were stashed away in his breast pocket. He had rolled two big fat marijuana joints and the cat was out of the bag that he had a helper – Mary Jane. She was the one who pushed the mower up and backwards and down and forwards. Duggy couldn't have done it alone. He was too zonked out of his pepper corned gourd.

On the average pay scale, Duggy's earnings came to about as high as a grasshopper's kneecap. As cheap as it was, his outlay on marijuana made serious fiscal inroads into his pittance pay. But Duggy was an addict, and with addicts it's only a matter of time. Soon he would be mine.

In order to accustom him to a life of crime, I started to spin my web. "Duggy," I ensnared, "I've got a present for you. I'll come by Sunday arvie and you can check it out. It's a surprise, man, but I promise you it's a *lekker* one." Hopefully Duggy's fantasizing about a pair of takkies would keep him *compos mentis* enough for me to begin changing his life. Drunkenness was his habitual way of contending with the boredom and loneliness of the weekend. Goodbye loneliness – hello oblivion.

The early bird catches the worm only because he gets up at sparrowsfart. I tried to make it as early as possible on that Sunday. It was too late. Sitting on his bed, the blast of the midday Afrikan sun that shot in as I toed open the door reflected both off the empty bottle and his watery ochre eyeballs. He didn't even blink. All he could do was stare at me with no recognition at all. A total blank. It was a hopelessly deluxe case of intoxication. Duggy was dead to the world.

I took a rain check on my visit hoping to pop in before Duggy managed another trip to the shebeen. The shebeen illicitly served up a muti that could turn the most pleasant of errant housemaids, and now a truant, into a glazy-eyed, paralyzed zombie that inebriation had glued to the gutter. Duggy had probably made it home on autopilot.

It was a long week till Sunday came around (hopefully together with Duggy). With fingers crossed, but not fully optimistic regarding his planned activities for his day of rest, I set out in the race against Duggy's throat lubricant. I won on a technicality: he, God knows how, somehow managed to stand up and walk. And so to work.

"Hey Duggy let's go to the teachers' staff room and make some coffee. Here, let me help you with the keys." Tick o' Locks — I was in. After a couple of hot sips of black coffee (there was no milk to cool it down), I announced in my most prophetic voice: "Duggy — it is time!"

I just smiled, ignored his querying glance and handed over his present. "I left one at home," I said. "I got two from the stable hands at the race course." Duggy opened his envelope and smiled, an opened-lip grin with his tongue protruding through the gap in his nonexistent front teeth. He closed the envelope and stuffed it in his pocket.

Hey! Hey! Hey! Gotcha, Douglas!

The envelope did not contain a lucky racehorse shoe but a quarter ounce of top grade marijuana. His illicit acceptance of this forbidden gift elevated me to the position of his supplier. The following week I presented him with the second envelope. He was soon to become dependent on me. Duggy and I were partners in crime. Shake on it.

He had the keys and, to keep up his end of the partnership, Duggy had to provide me with access to all and everywhere. From then on, most Sunday afternoons were spent by me, feet up on Obershmoober's desk, relaxing deeply into his high backed, big-shot chair and making random international phone calls to all and sundry.

"Hey, Duggy, I need a line please and what about some coffee and, please Duggy, without a million spoons of sugar." Duggy loved his coffee sweet. What was left of his teeth was dissolving as quickly as the sugar cubes. He used to laugh at my joke: *Question*: "Hey Duggy, how many sugars?" *Answer*: "Two in a cup, six in a jam tin." He would flick the lever marked Kommandant on the switchboard in the Secretary's office and then he was away and making coffee. I was away and dialing.

First, some random numbers to make a few new friends around the world. "Hello do you speak English? The Federal Republic of Germany? Fucking German! Auf Wiedersehen." Then I would make a couple of phone calls for Costas to Cyprus.

Megalomania had not drawn me to Obershmoober's office. It was not my favorite place to relax in — the sick room had a comfortable bed — but the interrupted view through the window of the long drive from the school gate, through the playing fields, would provide me with enough time to close up shop and skedaddle should anyone decide to come a-visiting on a Sunday. It also had some other attractions. The third desk drawer down on the right-hand-side contained Obershmoober's MA psychology thesis he had nearly finished working on. I thought it was interesting, but Costas opined that it was puerile. I discovered, discarded in the back of another desk drawer, a memo in Obershmoober's handwriting no less, pertaining to a certain Goon pedophile. On Costas' advice I sticky-fingered it.

In fact there was nothing I didn't go through. With Duggy's keys on hand, nothing was left unturned in my quest for knowledge. Cupboards with files, drawers with memos, abounded. The Goons' personal files were an enlightenment. I now understood the reason behind them being such a miserable bunch. They could never fathom out how the class would know their birthdays and invariably greet them with a disharmonised *Happy Birthday to You* in three languages, followed by the inevitable letdown: "Hey, Miss, how old are you?" 'Miss', who always tried to earn our trust with claimed honesty, lied to us, at least about her age.

Except for one place, everything was open to my scrutiny. The exception was the big wall safe adjacent to the secretary's office. They didn't trust Duggy with a key. It was in this safe, behind a fireproof, burglarproof steel door, the school's collection of silver trophies was kept together with the exam papers and test sheets. I needed a contingency plan.

A Roneo machine is a type of printing press with a simple technology. Stalag's Roneo machine was made by Gestetner. And it was on this Gestetner that the exam papers were printed. The liberal, blonde school secretary had to type out the exam on what is called a stencil. A stencil is made up of three layers of foolscap. First, you have a thin sheet of tissue paper that protects the second layer; a wax sheet that is perforated by the slamming of the typewriter keys. These perforations allow the ink to seep through onto the paper when printing. The third and final sheet is the backing. This is a proof sheet and a perfect facsimile of what is to be printed. After the stencil is attached to the elliptical drum, the top tissue and the backing are discarded. The wax sheet is wrapped around the drum. Clickety-clack, clickety-clack, the drum revolves and Roneoed exam sheets pop out, the fresh ink attacking the olfactory nerves.

Duggy was roped in at the end of term to help the secretary in running off the myriad examination sheets needed for investigating the progress, or, in some cases, the lack of progress, of each individual inmate. Part of his job description was to take care of the inky aspects of attaching the stencil to the drum. Liberal Blonde Secretary couldn't stand getting her fingers black. The tissue paper was ripped off, crumpled, and thrown into a cardboard carton, followed by the backing, with the secretary checking that this was done without exception. She was the boss. Oh, to lay one's hands on those backings – a passport to an A plus. The Goons may have been fools but they were not imbeciles. Many a schoolboy had scrummaged through the garbage bins vainly trying to locate a backing. The best they could ever come up with was some Afrikaans song-sheet backing:

*Vat jou goed en trek Ferreira, vat jou goed en trek.* Ray Charles sung it as *Hit the road Jack.*

The Goons had of course noted their indiscreet rummaging, which resulted in the cardboard box being invariably taken home by the secretary and spirited away in a fashion unbeknown to anybody.

Occasionally, and only occasionally, as not to take advantage of Secretary's liberal outlook, Duggy would, in-between wet ink sniffles, blow his nose on a torn-off sheet of tissue paper. A little later he would unscrumple the grungy piece of tissue and hold it up to the light. There it was, barely discernable, but nevertheless there – embossed in the tissue paper was my math exam. Highlighted with snot. "Not good enough, Duggy, try again please." Duggy went back to the drawing board and came up with a polite: "Please, Missy, can I have a piece to roll my twak… tobacco?" Having got the go-ahead, he carefully folded the tissue paper and stored it away in his pocket, later giving it to me in exchange for an envelope. We were off and running.

So far, of course, the off and running part of things was all in theory. Following Costas' advice that the best direction was the one of least effort and we shouldn't get involved, Duggy now had a new employer. I had more than generously enhanced his meager salary from the Upholder's private coffers. Duggy now worked for me — easy.

Years later I used to dreamily watch Duggy through the classroom window. My short attention span, aided by the continuous hum of the fluorescent light, had converted a history teacher's voice from a "... and the direction that South African history was to take would rest entirely on the whims of a *kaffirvoorlooper* ..." into a background "blah blah blah ..." and there was my man Duggy, who by now had been promoted to a tractor-driven lawnmower. Up and down he traversed into the sun, with his leatherette cap pulled over his eyes, and back again — this time the cap pushed back all the way to protect the rear of his head. Now he stops near the center of the field, putting his tractor into neutral and taking his Zippo lighter, fueled with petrol siphoned from his tractor's tank, and with a spate of huffing, sparks and puffing, he relights his brown paper joint. Engaging gear, off he goes, up and down, back into battle. A true Knight of Afrika.

# CHAPTER FOUR

I was late for my business appointment.

A secretary showed me into the boardroom where the Master of yester-eve and Stephen, of publishing company fame, were playing cards and occupied in reading each other's mind. They were wasting their time.

"Ah, there you are. Please tell Stephen that he has to *want* it to happen for *it* to happen."

No 'good morning'. That's the way it is with the rich; accordingly, I jacked up my price. I had things to do and places to go, so I got right down to brass tacks.

"How much is the rest of the manuscript worth to you? A hundred thousand?"

"A hundred thousand!" they gasped.

"Agreed," I said. "Now we've come to an arrangement about the figure …"

Master interrupted. "Are you an Israelite or something?"

"There are many beliefs," I told him. "I believe one has to pay a price for honesty. Nothing comes cheaply these days."

They closed the deal. "Okay, but it's nothing for nothing – no manuscript, no pay."

"You gentlemen certainly drive a hard bargain. I'll be honest with you; it's only due to my reduced circumstances that I'm willing to work for such a pittance. I'll contact you if I have something to report, but you can rest assured I've got an action plan. I have to start by tracking down a small black man called Duggy. He's our lead to the author of the manuscript."

Stephen stabbed me with a sharp eye. "What? Does he really exist?"

"That is precisely what I'm going to find out."

"How do you propose to do that?" They eyed me, half expecting psychic antennae to sprout from my head.

"First things first – I have to really want *it* to happen. Then I'm going to make an appointment with Chief Inspector Van der Merwe, the boxing referee."

Stephen spluttered. "You reckon he exists – in real life?"

"You'd better believe it old chap. You had better believe *it*."

The right thing to do is to always look busy, so I activated my dialing finger.

"Police Plaza – good morning. How can I help you?"

"Good morning. I'd like to speak with Inspector Van der Merwe."

"The Chief Inspector has retired. Can I put you through to someone else?"

"No thanks. Cheerio."

When all else fails the best last resort is to turn to technology. I turned my computer on and did a search for the Chief Inspector. More work for my finger. The internet came up with seventeen sites, among them the Dispatch Herald's home website. I clicked on *archives* and up popped:

*Chief Inspector Martinus van der Merwe will be retiring to his home and landscaped garden in Chatis Park when he reaches pension age in a month's time. He said: "I'm not going to idle away my time, but work in my garden and do some writing."*

*The only people who are happy to see him go are the criminal element in our society.*

*Inspector Van der Merwe turned down an offer to extend his term of duty. "I can now devote more of my time to finishing my book,* The Fall of Afrikaanderdom,*" he told reporters at a farewell party in his honor at Police Plaza.*

*"I am not abandoning ship but passing the helm over to a younger captain, so all those skolies out there had better still watch out."*

I dialed directory enquiries; there are two hundred and six Martinus van der Merwes listed.

"Chatis Park. Does that help you?"

"Sir, I have a Martinus van der Merwe on Bok-bok Drive."

"Yes, that could be it. Street number … damn … what number was that again? Help an old man …" I held my breath. Operators are not supposed to give out addresses.

"It's 22, Bok-bok Drive. Would you like me to connect you?"

"No thanks. Toodleloo."

I have always championed the direct approach so I set out for 22 Bok-bok Drive, Chatis Park. Peering over the myrtle berry hedge, I found what was probably the Inspector's house, compliments of the telephone company. A man was perspiratoryly working in the yard, turning over turf under the supervision of whoever was sitting on the shady front stoop – most likely the Inspector. The Chinese have a saying: The eye can never tire of three things: fire burning, water flowing and watching another man work.

This was no English country garden – the beware-of-the-dog sign on the gate made it quite clear. Posted in only one language: *pasop vir die hond*, a tarnished brass sign was on guard duty. If you did not *praat die taal* or speak the Afrikaans language, it was your own tough luck and just cause to be savaged by a Rhodesian Ridgeback.

I hailed over the gate, speaking in Afrikaans, taking a crack at applying a soothing balm to his Anglophobia, hoping he would be accommodating. *"Môre Meneer; hoe gaan dit met Meneer?"* I inquired of his well-being.

*"Wat die fok maak jy hier, jou fokking rooinek?"* He got up and ambled over to the hedge.

This redneck decided to revert to English in the hope that the Inspector would be less comfortable with his superlatives in that language.

"*Meneer,* everyone says you know a lot about boxing. I've come to ask you if you know a boxer called TapTap Bakateeny?"

He stared at me long enough to make me feel uncomfortable.

"No-fine. You must be psychic, *kêrel*, I've just now been thinking of that exact cheeky kaffir. Come in, come in. It's getting too hot now to be working outside. We'll drink some rooibos tea in the kitchen."

He ushered me, by way of the front yard, through the door into a gloomy hallway, and before coming in, yelled out: "Hey you! Silence! You carry on digging. When you're finished come round to the back for some tea."

He explained: "His name is Silence – he's deaf and dumb."

Well, that was news to me. If he was deaf, how would he know to carry on digging? And if he was dumb how could he have mumbled "*I see you HardSucker*" to me as I passed him along the garden path?

The retired Inspector put the kettle on to boil and shook out an estimated amount of rooibos from a paper bag into a teapot. "This stuff is a God send. Now you listen to me young *kêrel,* if you ever overdose on *biltong*, you try some of this stuff. Sit, sit. How can I help you?"

I sat. "TapTap the boxer is how you can help me."

"*Ja-nee.* You know *kêrel*, I have a very sad situation. I'm just right now writing a historical book on the reasons for what I call the 'collapse of Afrikaanderdom' … and it's full of lies. Man, how can I now confess to the whole world that it was *my* fault; even though I couldn't help it?

"The Soweto riots started in sympathy with the hell that broke out in NewBrightTin that afternoon after *that* boxer won *that* fight. There was a heck of a cock-up with the betting and the bookies couldn't pay out. The blacks went bananas, man. Remember that Biko was from NewBrightTin? And they were angry like wounded leopards. The ANC had planted *agents provocateur* in the crowds. It was their test run for Soweto.

"I was the referee of the fight and I had no choice. What could I have done, man? One of them was prostrated with heat exhaustion. I *had* to give the fight to TapTap. So there you have it. It was my decision that brought down the white regime in this country. If I only could get my hands on that kaffir today, I'll *donner* him.

"The funny thing was, he has a twin brother I once got my hands on. I sent him to jail for seven years for double manslaughter. He should have got the rope. His name was Douglas."

I shivered. "Who did he kill, *Meneer*?"

"Pour some tea, man, it looks like you have a temperature. I'll go and check my files."

I chose an enamel tin mug from the sink counter and poured myself some rooibos. The mug's metal rim, infused with heat from the boiling water, scalded my lips. I blew on it and managed a quick sip. Crikey Moses! It tasted horrible.

The Inspector returned. "What are you doing, man? Have you gone mad? That's the kaffir's cup you're drinking from!

"I found this in my files. Listen to this, man. Douglas Bakateeny killed a foreigner called DuBois, or something. Now get this. After three months in jail he just disappeared. Gone. People presume he escaped. To this very day it's a mystery.

"Now that was a tragic story if I ever heard one. It happened when they were demolishing all those houses in Brakston Park. Bakateeny was ripping the corrugated iron from the roofs and selling it to the *pondokkie* builders in the Townships. He had quite a racket going. The homeowners gave him the corrugated iron sheets for nothing.

"We don't know exactly what this DuBois character was doing there in the first place, but one of the loose iron sheets slid off the roof and decapitated him, chopping his head clean off. *Ja,* it rolled across the driveway and we found it under the hedge.

"He carried on walking, like a headless chicken, for a couple of steps. Just then the poor homeowner came with coffee for the workers and was scared out of his wits when he saw this headless man, blood pumping out of his neck, making his way down the driveway. He had a massive heart attack and died on the spot.

Killed by fright, I suppose you could say. *Ja-nee*, I felt sorry for him, man."

He looked at me directly. "Do I know you from somewhere? I never forget a face."

"I have to go now, *Meneer*. Can I come again some time? I'll take this tea out to Silence on my way," I told him.

"No-fine, *Totsiens kêrel.*"

Silence started digging again when he heard the front door opening. I walked over with the tea.

*"I see you Silence."*

*"I see you my Chief HardSucker."*

*"How do you know my name?"*

*"All the people talk about you and the magic you have in your head, my Chief."* He looked down into the mug and drank thirstily; deeply. *"Hauw – hyena urine!"*

*"It is the white man's bowel medicine, my brother ... Where is the dog?"*

*"Oh my Chief, some leopards took him one night."*

*"Hauw! Leopards in the big city?"*

*"Yes, my Chief, they are the black leopards that only come out at night."*

*"And where are they during the day?"*

*"They are buried deep, so I dig to loosen the earth for them. If the ground is hard they cannot get out at night, my Chief."*

*"Dig well, my cousin Silence."*

*"Go well, my Chief HardSucker."*

I did the only reasonable thing. I went back home and put my feet up with the manuscript. I skimmed through some of the stuff I'd already read and settled down with …

## On the House
***Children play and we learn about pedophiles***

### Part One

I was on my way to rendezvous with the gang one morning, when I came across my first dead body. It didn't occur to me that the man was in fact a corpse until later when I met up with Gee, who'd filled me in on his day's activities. It was what he mentioned in casual conversation around the gloomy kitchen table that germinated an inkling of a suspicion that something was untoward.

"Yes, and I threw some rocks at him and he didn't wake up, he didn't even move. Those people, man, they can sleep anywhere! Gee whizz man ..."

I knew, as trouble was my calling, that the little niggling or simmering at the back of the mind, which was feeding insatiably on my intuition, would inevitably drive me back to the spot. Yes, but this time not alone; I would let Gee tag along as my back-up. Fluffy Freckleton, because of his ginger freckles and the beginnings of a down soft, rusty steel-wool coloured moustache, our third Musketeer, was immediately deputized by Gee, as *his* back-up. Yippedeedoodah, the whole gang was going on a corpse hunt!

Gee, or Gerald Wizzner, which was his real name, as a toddler had referred to himself as 'Gee-whizz'. Initially endearing it might have been, indeed, with everybody thinking it rather cute, though, like all bad habits that stick and are hard to break, in latter years it drove his poor mother scatty. Gerald was named after his grandfather, who had gone up in Auschwitz smoke and his mother, a survivor from that same hell, was forever telling him to 'stop Gee-whizzing', as his name was Gerald after his grandfather of blessed memory.

Unfortunately, he lost control of his habit and his Gee-whizzing, which could not be contained, was coordinated into his everyday speech patterns. He Gee-whizzed this and Gee-whizzed that with a compulsive fanaticism that propelled it into every second sentence.

He was just a nervous kid; a second-generation holocaust survivor.

It was in his house, with drawn curtains and no lights on after dark, the day before the corpse hunt, when his father, Herr Doktor Herloff Wizzner, had approached me, requesting my help in trying to preserve what little was left of his and his wife's sanity.

"Ve had boys like you in zhe camps. I haf been vatching you; you can help us, ja?"

I didn't know if that was a compliment, or what.

Their horrors of years past, which could not be cast off and were being relived on a daily basis, had been intensified by the young blades of the neighborhood, who were persecuting Herr Doktor's family by continuously victimizing, and without any pleaded-for respite, insistently playing *tok-tokkie* on their front door. Their routine banging on the door before running away left the house's inhabitants in a shaking terror as they re-experienced that night of long ago when Nazi storm troopers hammered on their door in Leipzig and carted them away. He, to mix concrete in shunting yards by day, repairing the destruction of the previous night's Allied bombing; and his wife to Auschwitz, to die of disease or starvation, if the selection didn't get her first.

Herr Doktor was not a doctor but a dentist. He'd promised me free orthodontal work in remuneration if I succeeded in arresting his nightly anxiety attacks brought on by, what he termed, "zhose loutish dumkopfs."

He had graduated from the Leipzig College of Dental Medicine before the outbreak of war, but was now employed as a dental technician. Molding false teeth and dental plates in a dentist's surgery during working hours and moonlighting as an orthodontist, utilizing the weekend when the dentist was away, was how he put bread on the table.

I looked up at Gee, who was finishing some of that bread in the form of a peanut butter sandwich. He swallowed the last of it and gave a wide grin to advertise his dad's prowess. The mess of entangled wires and hooks, held together by a phalanx of rubber bands, along with the unswallowed rubble of a white bread and chunky peanut butter sandwich, could only have been modeled on a Dresden shunting yard after an intense Allied attack.

The payment I'd extracted in remuneration from Gee and his family in return for my friendship was Gee's unzealous attachment to his homework – letting me copy it at every turn of the pencil sharpener. He was not an overly bright boy and his borderline dullness was reflected in my grades. It was less than adequate, but it would have been churlish of me to take advantage of Herr Doktor's generous proposition.

"Thanks, but no thanks," I had told him. "This one's on the house."

"Ja, ve had boys like you in zhe camps. You vill do, ja?"

"Ja," I told him.

The three-man gang set out on the hunt. We crossed Ascot Road, with houses flanking one side, and the nether reaches of the racecourse on the other. A chain-link fence separated the knee-high Afrikan growth from the road and the well-nurtured gardens. Gee bravely led the way as he knew the exact spot, but drew back when we approached the hole in the fence. We could make out the 'sleeping' person, splayed face down on the pathway, which sliced through the Afrikan brush, and accessed a shortcut across the course.

Gee crawled through the hole after me, then, with evaporated bravado, stayed put, gripping onto the fence near the escape hole for security thus leaving the final approach up to me. Fluffy Freckleton didn't even make it through the fence, which was probably a good thing, making it easier to delegate him to go and knock on a door and ask if he could phone the police when the time came.

I ratified my earlier inkling that he was dead the instant I touched his shoulder. I rolled the stiff body over and was presented with an unpretty sight, best undescribed; suffice it to say that it looked as if both the blunt, as well as the sharp, end of an axe or hatchet had been taken to the face; definitely not the sort of injuries caused by Gee's pebble tossing.

"He's dead," I announced.

Gee took it rather badly. "Gee-whizz, gee-whizz, gee-whizz, man. I've stoned a man to death. Gee-whizz! I mean to death, man. It's because of me. Oh my gee-whizz – killed. I've killed a man!"

"Gee. Stop gee-whizzing," I told him. And to Fluffy: "Go phone the police."

I wasn't privy to the exact version of the story a panic-stricken Gee's father was presented with or how much he managed to dredge up of the truth of the matter from Gee's hysterical gee-whizzes, but years later, when he once again approached me for some assistance, he warned me to lay off.

"Last time you vent too far, ja? You dit not haf to stone that dumkopf of a *tok-tokkie* player to death. Zhis is not gut, ja?"

"Huh?"

I didn't bother to rectify Herr Doktor's misconception. How could I possibly come clean after all this time? Little did the good doctor know his *tok-tokkie* problem had been solved quite amiably, when on that Saturday night of long ago with the gang finalizing plans for our evening's activities, I had announced: "Let's not play *tok-tokkie* any more. It's too scary."

## On the House
## Part two

Everybody knows the devil makes work for idle hands, but being essentially a lazy person I hoped to outwit him. I decided to kill two birds with one stone.

To all intents and purposes I'm the most genial of blokes, but fear gathers itself in the most innocuous of places, and as I weave together the parts of this story and braid them into a tale of despair, it will become easily apparent that, if the need arises, I have the ability, know-how, training and above all, expertise – the fruit of my experience – to turn most people's lives into a dischord, by skillfully plucking at the strings of fear we all have buried so deep, that I oftentimes amuse myself in seeing how close to the target I can actually come when stabbing into the dark netherworld of the individual psyche.

The people I hold in awe are few and far between. Among them can be counted Ivan the Terrible, Hannibal Lecter and Herr Doktor Herloff Wizzner, part-time orthodontist from Leipzig; or was that Dresden now? For years, fear had been his constant cohort and it was only out of habit that he still walked hand in hand with it, resigning himself to the apprehensive and unwelcome companionship of a bullying friend: no more than that.

Our Herr Doktor was a graduate of the Seen-it-Done-it School of Horror and Suffering and was immune to the social consequences of his actions. There remained of him no substance, only the hint of a man with cardsharped emotions and trepidations. A wraith in the shadows, lurking in dusky doorways, neither here nor there. Very scary.

Over the years he had begun to confide in me more and more. So, when he came to me with a problem that he laid on the table, I listened, for who knows when someone might learn something from others' troubles? I listened, I thought, and I laughed out loud as I announced: "We are going to kill two birds with one stone."

"Ja, zhis could be possible. I haf seen zhis done vith vun bullet, but vith more zhen two people. But zhis is no laughing matter, ja?" His German accent got so strong that it was an effort to work out what he was saying. "I vill tell you somezhing, my young friend: six is my lucky number. I vas born on zhe 6th of June, ja-ja, zhat is zhe sixth month, and I vas zhe number six child from six children.

"I vas also number six in line vhen Hauptman Wenglar stood us up to show off his vonderful marksmanship. Ve vhere standing zo close togezher zhat zhe Herr Hauptman set up a new record. Five men fell in front of me – all from vun bullet. Ja-ja. He vas so happy zhat he let me live – six alvays vas a lucky number for me ... ja-ja." He sighed again. "Zhere is nothing to laugh about."

"You're right Herr Doktor. But now, may I tell you a story?"

"Please-*bitte*."

I told him my story. We both laughed at the outcome. I raised a smug eyebrow to milk some comment or response.

"*Dumkopf* – I am not laughing vith you, but *at* you. I knew boys like you in zhe camps. Vhy don't you just kill zhem, ja?"

"I'm not allowed to."

"*Vundebaar* ..." His idea of killing two birds with one stone was more in the line of: A murder of crows – the advertisers of doom. "... So you vill tell me your story from zhe beginning, vunce again, ja? I vill listen."

So this is the story vunce again. *O what tales these mortal men weave ... etc.*

"Herr Doktor, I will lay out the parts for you, with all their facts, in an organized and precise manner, as I know that to be your particular preference. I can easily skip over irrelevant questions, such as why has the Obershmoober-commandant, the respected principal of the school ... I see you shudder when I mention that name. If it's easier for you I'll refer to him as Fat Rat."

"Zhe school vhat you jokingly call the Stalag is nothing like the vun I vas in, and you must believe me, zhat your Obershmoobercommandant is nothing like my Obershmoobercommandant vas. Ja, I zhink zhat Fat Rat vould be more suitable under zhe circumstances, even zough it is inadequate."

"Ja," I agreed. (Herr Doktor's 'ja-ing' was getting nearly as bad as his son's 'Gee-whizzing') "... And skipping over the whys and wherefores of Fat Rat allowing the Pedophile to go so far as he has, though he must be aware of what is happening under his very jowls – as pedophiles act in recognizable patterns, we ..."

"You vill tell me about zhis *recognizable patterns* zhing. Ve must have zhe full picture, ja?"

I gave him the Pedophile Lecture.

"Pedophiles select their victims from the weaker links in our society. They find their easy prey in emotionally damaged children, from broken families and the like." Under the circumstances, I didn't think it was wise to include the children of holocaust survivors. They also fell into the *emotionally damaged* category.

"Pedophiles start by instigating rumors and promoting malicious chitchat about perverse acts in which they and their victim have allegedly participated. The victim soon learns, at his or her expense, that any protest of denial is quickly adopted as a focal point for jokes and raggings by cruel schoolboys and only aggravates the misery and amplifies the horrid state of affairs. On another level, the wretched victim's inadequate protests of innocence all go unacknowledged, as everyone recognizes the whole thing is a lot of uncorroborated hogwash anyway.

"Our Pedophile, a figure of authority, has gone so far as to publicly ban the circulation of these stories, ostensibly to protect his poor victim from unfair anguish. But all of this is part and parcel of his ploy to feed the dark denizens of his sick psyche, which unharness control and drive the diabolic sicko to swoop and to take his pleasure.

"There are variations on this theme but, when the Pedophile finally pounces, the poor abused boy is left to contend with an inevitable set of new rumors, albeit true this time, that are now disregarded as being yet another round of groundless tittle-tattle, whose exhausted entertainment value has already been wrung dry, even by the most deplorable of wags. Besides, Pedophile had forbidden any idle chatter linking the victim to perversions. The poor boy, already having experienced the bitter results of attempted denial, feels, and rightly so, that going so far as to cry for help by admitting guilt would, at best, be met with bored indifference, and so he is sadly left with no recourse but to withdraw further within himself and to suffer his denigration in silence. And that, in a nutshell, is how the Pedophile operates.

"Yes, and sadly enough, all of this, the good old principal, Fat Rat, knew was happening; it was with his tacit say-so."

"And all zhis you know for a fact, ja?"

"Yes, all this I know for a fact. I have an incriminating memo, in Fat Rat's handwriting nonetheless, in safekeeping."

"But vhy? Vhy does he let zhis carry on?"

The answer to that was obvious to anyone who had made a study of Fat Rat's egotistical megalomania.

"Despite all his failings, our Pedophile is a brilliant science teacher and he can guarantee a hundred percent pass-rate in the matriculation examinations, and this, Herr Doktor, is Fat Rat's wet dream."

"Vet dream — to hell. Zhis is a *Gott-verdampt* nightmare."

The Jabotinsky Day School substantiated its reputation as one of the best schools in the southern hemisphere by maintaining an untarnished matriculation record. Through the many years of its existence every matriculant had added to the school's sterling character, with nary a failure. This was no accident. It was accomplished by giving the boot to any pupil with a projected malfunction; maybe those who were not scholastically enough inclined, but definitely to those who were just plain stupid. For some, the yellow brick road of education was potholed. They were generally frogmarched to the back door and unceremoniously hurled out onto the hard asphalt of life, to limp along for a short while before they vanished into one of its sinkholes. Phut. Gone forever.

"Fat Rat is under tremendous pressure to maintain an impeccable record. The board of governors has made it quite clear that his and his family's livelihood ride on the prolongation of these historic scholastic accomplishments."

At the end of the school calendar year, Fat Rat's jowls agitated more than normal. The matric exams were looming over the horizon and the chronic heat rash brought on by the incessant rubbing of the knot of his tie, which was hidden under the sweaty folds of his double chin, began to play up more than usual as he expended himself, belly flopping from pupil to pupil, egging them on with cries of: "Hurry up boy – there's learning afoot."

I paused to gather my thoughts.

"And zo?"

It seemed Herr Doktor was getting bored with my rambling on, so I decided to head straight for the core of the matter.

"And so, Herr Doktor, our saving grace is Gee's ..." For once I was at a loss for words. How could I diplomatically inform a father that his son was intellectually challenged and that, in the scholastic department, Gee's elevator didn't quite reach the top floor? All this, without insult. I took a deep breath and came out with it: "And so, our saving grace is that Gee is not university material."

"Ja-ja, zhis I know. He gets it from his mother's side."

I exhaled, fluttering the slip of paper he had previously laid on the table – the root of Gee's dad's crisis.

He picked it up. "But vhat about *zhis*?" he bemoaned. It was Gee's compulsory call-up papers to the army. He had been conscripted to SAI-12 (Upgtn), the Twelfth South African Infantry Brigade in Uppington. I felt sorry for Gee; there was no way the poor soul was going to make it. I mean, what did the military authorities want with someone like him anyway?

Herr Doktor probably picked up on my question telepathically, for he gave me the answer. "Cannon fodder ..." he choked. "Cannon fodder. I vill not let zhis happen. Ve haf lost too many in our family ... *Gott-in-Himmel!* He is zo young and still in braces." He broke down and began sobbing tearlessly. I couldn't even offer him a tissue.

He was right. Herr Doktor had, over the years, all in the name of orthodontics, spot-welded so many additional pieces of metal to Gee's teeth the enemy's radar would target him in no time at all. Herr Doktor had undertaken postgraduate study in the Arbeit Macht Frei School of Dental Medicine and in a moment of honesty he had once admitted that the end of Gee's orthodontic treatment was nowhere in sight. "Zhere is alvays vork to be done in zhe mouth, ja?" But it went deeper than that.

The routine Allied bombing of railway junctions had fortuitously provided him with enough forced reconstruction labor to justify him being kept alive; and the day Herr Doktor finally crowbarred off Gee's braces would be the day that he finished the work he'd begun in Dresden (or Leipzig) and give an opening for the devil to take care of his idle hands. He had to hold onto Gee – his life – no matter what the cost.

When I presented some of our options, Herr Doktor composed himself. I described for him the army call-up train as it pulled into a station with brown uniformed railway police lining the tracks and the platform, all on the lookout for runners. He turned pale and again lost his composure.

I went on to explain that as the train pulled in, draft dodgers would leap off and make a run for it, fanning out. The alert railway police trapped some, but others would make it past the cordon to be hunted down by military police in pinball alleys and billiard halls and on recapture, loaded onto the next army train from which they would once again bale out at the first opportunity. But some evaded recapture; like fish through a net, it was the small ones that got away.

"*Nein!* I knew cowvards zhat jumped from trains to escape zheir fate, and zhe operative vord is *knew*. None zhat jumped vere ever seen again."

This led us to the final solution: deferment.

As Gee was not university material, it would be impossible to wangle a deferment on the grounds that he was a medical student. But there was one loophole and that was how I was going to kill the two birds with one stone. Anyone who was kept back a year to redo his matric was given a deferment from service. All Gee had to do was to miserably fail his matric exams.

"Ja-gut, zhis takes care of both Gee-whizz's problem and zhe Fat Rat as vell. But vhat about *Shweinhund* Pedophile?"

"That, my dear Herr Doktor Wizzner, may take some time. But when that time comes – it's on the house."

I certainly wasn't going to put the manuscript down now. I carried on reading. The next chapter I chose wasn't numbered, just named:

## Dungbeetle

***The Upholders go into action.***
***Pedophile becomes a reborn Xtian.***
***Duggy helps make dynamite in school science lab.***

*Factae non Verbae* was the proud motto of our Upholder School or as my instructor DuBois' minced idiom put it: "oyiniaucket, ull yoinge ouyoack" (for crying in a bucket, pull your finger out your jack).

Deciphering DuBois' speech patterns was, at the least, confusing, if not a trifle trying. He communicated through a metal grommet surgically implanted into his neck. The Darwinists of our acquaintance had a field day around the stainless steel implant. They proclaimed DuBois a living specimen; a proof of evolution. Citing Darwin's theory, that unlike the apes, we have the capability of using our mouths as an auxiliary tool, they took DuBois' case under consideration.

Once, prior to inserting a detonator into the plastic explosives he was dabbling with, DuBois had felt the charge needed repositioning. Requiring both hands to make the necessary adjustments, he temporarily held the detonator between his lips Lucky Strike-fashion. (A monkey is incapable of working out the logistics of utilizing his mouth to hold the detonator.) Unfortunately, he struck it unlucky when the detonator untimely exploded and a surprised DuBois was left *sans* tongue and part of his lower mandible. The consequence of his folly is that he can no longer hold anything in his mouth, and due to this reversion of nature, Mr Darwin's disciples refer to DuBois as the only man who has managed to make a monkey out of himself.

Some said he would have made a master ventriloquist if he had done something to improve his enunciation. Is this what you have to put up with if you wanted an instructor you could love and respect?

Yes. DuBois was my loved and respected practical work master and instructor.

## Practical Work — Mid term Project

The wake was over. After the last revelers left we waltzed in. Hidden behind balaclavas and carrying all the necessary equipment, DuBois led the way. I followed with Costas conscripted as our rear guard. Duggy, our driver/lookout was out front, ready to act as our backup, or backout if things got a little dirty. The Upholders were going into action.

Pedophile, who had drunk himself into a sorrowful semi-stupor, mourning the sad loss of his dog earlier that day, couldn't shift from his bar stool let alone manage a confused belch before DuBois swiftly strode across the room and chloroform-padded him. Following our well-rehearsed plans, I cleared the bar top onto which he was unceremoniously dumped by DuBois and Costas.

At strategic points around the contours of the limp body we swiftly screwed hooks into the varnished wood. After his trousers and underpants were slipped down, he was strapped, via the hooks, to the bar top. With restraints across his neck, torso, ankles and wrists, he was incapacitated – at our mercy.

While waiting for Pedophile to come round, we wiled away our time. Costas poured drinks all around (Coke for me, brandy and Coke for DuBois. Nothing was sent out to Duggy – he was driving). DuBois manicured his cuticles with his nine-inch double-edged dirk; he endearingly referred to it as his *Patrushka*. Costas plucked his over-sprouted nostril hairs in the bar mirror. I left them to their personal grooming and immersed my mind into a re-run of the events of the past couple of days.

It had all begun at the hardware shop with a shopping list drawn up by my 'dad'.

"Sir, please ... Dad wants some hydrochloric acid to open the maid's drains; it's all blocked up again." No problem.

Then a quick skedaddle down the road to the Art Supply Place.

"Please Sir, please can I have a bottle of nitric acid for etching copper ... and please Sir, Dad asks if he can have it from the chemically pure stock?" No problem.

The last stop was the main hurdle. Pharmacists are aware of the inherent, lethal potential of glycerin.

"Please Sir." ... Easy does it ... "Please, do you have glycerin for blowing soap bubbles?" Leaving 'Dad' out of it, I imagined up an Aunt Sophie: "Aunt Sophie says she'll teach us how." No problem.

With purchases in hand, all that that remained was to purloin a feather pillow from the sofa.

There was no doubt in my mind that the GWEQ of BP would note the pillow's absence, and after profuse denials on my part and repeated claims of innocence, I was sent down with an "it cannot just disappear" to the servants' quarters to see if the maid had stolen it. The Queen never went down there herself. She claimed the solid gaseous anomaly that made up the unique atmosphere of the servants' quarters couldn't sustain unconditioned organisms.

The peculiar smell, common to the maid's room but foreign to the rest of Afrika, was the impregnable divide, an invisible barrier that separated race from race. Attempts to cross it were made only by the courageous. They experimented with holding their breath until dizziness drove them out. Breathing though the mouth to save the olfactory was unsatisfactory. The aroma permeated the nasal passages and took up residence. No amount of blowing and Kleenex could remove the microbic squatters, though a nasal inhalation of a warm solution of salt and bicarbonate of soda has been known to neutralize them. For the brave of heart and soul the only way to cross the great divide of Afrika was to step in through the unpainted door of the maid's room, inhale deeply, exhale and inhale once again, melding and becoming one with, and part of, Afrika – alive.

Peculiarly enough, the strange phenomenon was that *they* thought *our* houses also had a funny smell (or so we were told).

On Sunday, with Duggy acting as my ancillary force, the school's well-equipped science lab, with its beakers and mixing rods, was transformed into a bomb factory. Guy Fawkes would have been proud of us. We were upping the ante. His explosive of choice was gunpowder; we were making dynamite.

After clearing a workspace on the floor (Costas: nothing can fall further than the floor). I gingerly decanted four parts nitric acid to five parts sulphuric into a gigantic beaker. The fumes rising from the solution were hideously potent and highly volatile, so it was Duggy's job to stir the concoction with a glass rod. After making sure I'd established eye contact with Duggy, I strictly forbade him from smoking or turning on the light. The slightest spark would leave a mess of Duggy, half the school building and myself.

I had buried the beaker up to its rim in a picnic cool box packed with ice. Ensconced this way, the ice kept the solution from reaching a critical heat level as I added the penultimate ingredient – the glycerin. Duggy, now redelegated, punctured the pillow and collected the feathers as I took over the stirring of the viscous liquid, taking the utmost care not to inadvertently bang the sides of the beaker with the mixing rod. Peering at the calibrations, it appeared that I now had nearly a litre of nitroglycerine. It was about as unstable as a premenstrual sixteen-year-old. The slightest of mishaps would be our introduction to *Bab el* Kingdom Come. Duggy had the honor of adding the final ingredient, the feathers, to the nitroglycerine and the sweating mush was stuffed into some empty cardboard toilet rolls collected from the boys' cloakrooms.

We planted a detonator, a left over firecracker from Guy Fawkes' Day, into the top of each cardboard tube, and *Voilà* – we had made dynamite.

Later we timed our stroll in the park behind Pedo's house. We knew from previous recces that Pedo's border collie Diggidy – short for Hot Diggidy Dog – would be taking his constitutional and crap on the public lawn.

"Here! Fetch, Diggidy!" The canine's timing and coordination were superb. The fizzing, twirling stick of dynamite was caught in mid-flight as Diggidy catapulted himself into the air and snapped at the angel of death. The poor canine's last act on earth was a damn good imitation of a Chinese dragon dog when smoke puffed out of both his ears and nostrils as the small charge reverberated through his soft upper palate and shuddered the poor beast's brain into oblivion.

The wind blew away some residual shards of toilet roll, leaving absolutely no trace as to the cause of the dog's demise. DuBois proficiently did what he had to do, and then we meandered off, leaving Duggy to loiter and keep an eye on things from afar.

Everything had started according to plan. Pedo was alerted to the scene and probably, due to his anguish and grief at his pet's passing, did not note anything else untoward. The dog, presumed dead of a stroke, was wrapped in an old blanket and buried under the driveway in the eternal shade of a blue blossoming Jacaranda.

And it was back to reality. Pedo's moans of regaining consciousness alerted me to my position. Bewilderment was superceded by horror as he became more aware of his predicament. The screams of utter fear that welled up from the depths of his lungs were shut off as his eyeball skidded to a halt on the needlepoint of DuBois' Patrushka. He was incapacitated and his only resort was to involuntary void himself. An earthy odor permeated the room as Pedo's sphincter erupted and left him lying in the warm effluent of a beery BM.

Now was the time to show him the light at the end of the tunnel — that faint glimmer of hope. Accordingly, Costas reassured him that our motives were not murder but mayhem. "Just something to act as a reminder to desist in the abuse of little boys." No, we weren't going to kill him, only teach him a jolly good lesson. Costas' additional reassurances, as he anaesthetized Pedo's scrotal region with ethyl-chloride spray, that it would be a painless procedure, didn't seem to put him any more at ease. He graduated into hell as DuBois, without faltering, deftly snapped a thick rubber band around the root of Pedo's scrotal sack. With a grommety, "or-yin..." (For crying in a cloudburst; It is time. Say goodbye to your balls Dungbeetle) accompanied by a flick of his double edged dagger the deed was done. He displayed the trophy on the point of his blade and with another swanky flick sent it on its way. Pedo's eyes followed the parabolic flight pattern of his testicles, which ended with a plop in the ice bucket.

His eyes rolled up into the back of his cranium as his psyche shut down, preferring oblivion to reality. After another round of Coke and brandy, he reawoke to his nightmare and would have screamed and screamed and screamed had Costas not preempted him by stuffing a wet bar towel into his mouth.

DuBois: "O-yin..." (For crying out loud we can't leave him lying like this with his finger up his jack. Let's squash the dungbeetle.)

Me: "No! We are not allowed to kill him." Too late – with another flick of the blade, Pedo's life support system, the elastic band, twanged across the room.

Me: "He's losing blood fast. He's hemorrhaging. He'll bleed to death!"

Costas: "Quick – remember *factae non verbae* – we have to get him to the hospital post haste!"

Costas stuffed the bar towel from Pedo's mouth down Pedo's pants before buckling them up; hopefully this would soak up the blood. Patrushka came into play for the final time that evening as DuBois slashed Pedo's bindings. Pedo was propelled to the car clutching the ice bucket.

Duggy, getting the go ahead from DuBois: *"All-a-ack* (Ball that jack!)" revved the engine and took off like a bat out of hell.

## Theory

Theory is theory and I had to slog through a lot of it. It was none other than Costas, the mastermind of theories, who took me under his all-encompassing wing. It was at the Great White Elephant Queen of Brakston Park's adamancy that my Father had to step down as my sex educator. Costas, the devout Roman Catholic, was to be his understudy. She insisted it was primarily for my own safety. She sat in on the first lesson.

When Costas explained that Mommies' babies are put in their stomachs through the same passageway (position) by which they leave, the GWEQ of BP swept out of the room in embarrassment, leaving me to his own devices.

After continuing with a: "We are of a day and age when explicitness can be excused when relating to the matters of 'him' and 'her'," he warmed up with establishing that women are tantamount to untouchables when suffering their lunar assignations. Apparently we see in their taintedness the bloody results of our own impending castration. Muttering something about *vagina dentate*, he continued to expand on the subject of pheromonal graveyards and the rot rate of unburied pheromone carcasses. Then we swept onto the impractibility of intimate deodorants. This diatribe progressed to an oral quiz.

Q: What did the blind man say when he accidentally walked into the fish shop?

A: ...

Through an ajar door, from the realm of the eavesdropper, the regal: "I am at the end of my tether" terminated my sex education as far as Costas was concerned. He did manage to mutter something about *premenstrual lunacy* before he felt it was wise to vacate the premises for a period.

The only bit of royal advice I ever received from the

Great White Elephant Queen of Brakston Park relating to the subject of 'him' and 'her' was that my hormones were evolving and certain changes were taking place in my body. To keep this phenomenon under control, she advocated a regular daily application of underarm deodorant.

In Upholder School, creative writing, as an aspiration, was encouraged. Following is an essay, a poem and a play I've transcribed from my composition book.

## Fear

We have to learn to knock out fear and prevent it from becoming the middleman, demanding its percentage of our day-to-day existence. We pay no dues to fear. It cannot prevail upon us as it has no personal consequence except to be utilized as a tool – an open check, endorsed to deposit terror in our enemies' minds.

The intrigue of playing Russian roulette with someone's conscious and subconscious I find to be enthralling. I imagine that winding a string around the equatorial line of the brain's hemispheres thus improvising a yo-yo of the mind, then playing loop-the-loop with the psyche cannot be considered recess time activity.

The theory of escorting someone through the tunnel of terror until the warmth of loosened bowels is the only comfort against the coldness clutching at their very beings, when a jerk of the string turns on the light at the end of the tunnel, illuminating a last hope of hopes for salvation, then another yo-yo jerk transforms the light of redemption into a thundering express train bearing down into the victim's psyche, finally smashing it into smithereens, is not only captivating but something we can utilize in our practical work.

A final quote: "Ha – I laugh in the face of danger," sums it up.

Grade: 3/10

Here is the poem:

**Medical File**
**A poem by Quentin Locke**

*I told my doctor:*
*"El Doctore,*
*I will hold you partially responsible for my life."*
*He refused to operate.*
*Then:*
*"El Doctore,*
*I will hold you partially responsible for my death."*
*He flicked open the blade*
*of his Swiss army knife.*
*I told my doctor:*
*"El Doctore,*
*I will hold you partially responsible for my life."*
*He refused to operate.*
*Then:*
*"El Doctore,*
*I will hold you partially responsible for my death."*
*He cut out my wart.*

And finally the play:

**Act 1**

Cast: Dungbeetle, sister superior, three nurse nuns, doctor, two white-coated porters, The Great White Elephant Queen of Brakston Park.

Props: ice bucket, set of testicles.

Scene: The curtain rises on the emergency room of The Sisters of the Holy Virgin Mothers Hospital. Dungbeetle bursts in holding onto an ice bucket. He is obviously distraught.

Dungbeetle: Help, oh G*d please help, I'm bleeding. They've cut them off. My balls. My balls – here – in the ice bucket!

Sister Superior: Stand back, sisters. Block your ears and hold firm. Remember the first rule.

Nurse nun: Yes – hear no evil. But is he?

Sister Superior: Presumably the man is mad. He's obviously lost his marbles.

Dungbeetle: Yes! My marbles – oh – my marbles – oh help, please ...

Sister Superior: Come Sisters, join hands in prayer. (The Sisters clasp hands.) Let us pray. Dear Lord, please help this man. Return to him his lost marbles.

Three Nurse Nuns: Amen. Hallelujah and Hallelujah!

Sister Superior: Yes Sisters – Hallelujah and double Hallelujah! Please Lord, show this man your holy light.

Three Nurse Nuns: Amen. Amen!

Sister Superior: Yes! Amen and double amen.

(The doctor examines Dungbeetle and his testicles are found to be intact.)

Dungbeetle (incomprehendingly examining himself): My balls ... I don't believe it. How could it be? A miracle – my balls are back! Thank you, thank you, thank you Lord for giving them back. Yes! I have seen the light.

Doctor (aside; but overheard by Sister Superior): If it's a miracle, it's probably only of a minor sort, judging by the size of his balls that is.

Sister Superior (shocked): Doctor! (pause) Do you think he's a total lunatic?

Doctor (peering into the ice bucket): Yes Sister, undeniably. Call the SPCA if you will. (Shows Sister Superior the dog's testicles that he has discovered in the ice bucket.)

(The porters accompany/escort Dungbeetle to the

closed ward for sedation and observation. He is wheeled out, flanked by the men in white coats. The outer world's last view of him is with one hand cupping his privates and the other raised high, with fingers splayed, straining to touch the Lord's light from on high. His eyes rotate in different directions.)

Dungbeetle: The Lord has shone his light upon me! I have been chosen to witness his miracles, Hallelujah!

(The doors of the emergency room swing shut. He's gone. Exit Dungbeetle.)

Sister Superior and Three Nurse Nuns (in a four part harmony): Hallelujah ... Hallelujah ... Hallelujah.

(pause)

Great White Elephant Queen of Brakston Park (offstage): Good riddance to bad rubbish.

*Curtain.*

# CHAPTER FIVE

I phoned Stephen and hit him with it. "I'm going to need an extra ten big-ones for unforecasted expenses."

A frosty "What for?" blew down the line, via the Tundra.

"Unforecasted expenses. I need what we call a triple pee – a professional psychological profile – of this character we're looking for."

"Why?"

I switched ears to avoid frostbite.

"I've made some headway, but for me to establish contact with him on the psychic web, I need a fuller picture. The triple pee will fill in the blanks of a very complicated mindset."

"Ten grand is a very expensive paint by number. Exorbitant you might say, don't you think?"

"Yes, but the best costs – I can probably get a ten percent discount for cash ..."

Now the ball was in his court and I could sense him bouncing it around. Men like him take much pleasure in driving hard bargains and his return lob had its demands.

"Okay. You've got the money coming to you, but first you have to do something for me."

"And that is?" I sensed what he wanted, but I played the game through.

"I want you to do to me what you did to Freddy."

"To read your mind?"

"Yes. Just like you did to Freddy. Exactly. Without any gobbily goop thrown in. Can you do that?"

"Only if you really want it to happen I can. It all depends on you."

"That sounds like gobbily goop to me if I've ever heard it. Come over to my place now, let's see what you can do."

So that was Stephen – hook, line and sinker.

No 'hello, how are you?' from him. Everything was typical, with no unexpected offerings of a coffee or something cold to drink. I just can't get over the rich. The stinkwood dining table was cleared, with decks ready for action. Two of them, unopened packs of bicycle cards with seals still intact, one red and one blue, lying in front of a seated Stephen. I stood in the doorway.

"Good morning to you, Stephen," I coaxed.

Fat chance.

"Well, let's see you get down to it. Remember – no gobbily goop. Exactly as you did with Freddy."

I leant against the doorway and began my spiel. "Clear your mind, Stephen. Don't even talk.

"I chose to use cards with Freddy, so he could concentrate on something he was familiar with; an easily recognizable image for him to raise in his mind's eye. I'll run through what Freddy did while you follow the actions with the cards.

"First, as now, I never touched the cards or came close to them. Freddy broke the seals on both decks and shuffled them thoroughly."

Stephen did as Freddy had done. He shuffled, then selected a deck for me to use by pointing at it. He chose the blue one. The red one was placed aside.

"Now take a card from the blue deck in front of you. Slide the card out of the deck and keep it face down on the table at all times. Slip it out, from wherever you choose. Good. Now I'm going to turn around and you must peek at your card. Please remember it. You've done that? Put the card back on the deck and cut it in two. Replace the bottom half on the top and square the deck up. Cut the deck again … and again, and square it up. If you would like to cut some more, go ahead. Are you happy? If so, I'll turn around."

I looked at him. "Stephen, after shuffling and deciding on a deck, you chose a blue card and replaced it in the deck. After cutting, I don't know how many times, you lost its location. It's somewhere in there and you're the only person in the whole wide world who knows which card it is; if you haven't forgotten it by now, that is. If you recall, I even asked you if you were happy. Everything was fair and square. Am I correct?

"In that case, take up the red deck, the one you set aside, and look through it. Find the same card in it you just chose from the blue one and place it face down on the table. But wait till I turn around … Finished? Good."

I turned to face Stephen again and approached the table for the first time. "One final question before I read your mind. What was *I* doing while you were doing this? Nothing. Right?

"I want you to use the red card you found, which is now face down on the table, as an image. Lift it up into your mind's eye and I will look through the blue deck and see if I can pick out your chosen card. I will run through them and see if any particular card speaks to me, so to speak."

So saying, I lifted up the blue deck for the first time and began to look through it, trying to pick up a telepathic image from Stephen. I glared at the deck then I glared at Stephen, who glared back at me, trying very hard to transmit. I closed my eyes and counted softly to five; opened them, drew a card from the blue deck and placed it face down on the table next to its red companion.

Stephen's hand shot out to turn the card over but I stopped him. "Yours first, please."

He flipped over his card, a five of clubs, and then flipped over mine. They didn't match. It was a five of spades. Close, but not close enough for the 10,000 jackpot.

"I'm sorry, Stephen, but it seems you didn't want *it* to happen enough for *it* to happen. Perhaps you're subconsciously fighting *it*, because success will cost you 10,000."

Of course, Stephen asked if we could try again. We went through the same, but this time, he revealed a queen of diamonds.

He hopefully turned over the second card. Yes! A matching queen of diamonds.

Well, well, well.

"Well, here's your 9,000."

"I thought we'd agreed on ten."

"It's in cash. I get a ten percent discount, as agreed."

Go figure the rich.

## The proof is in the pudding

### *I reach my journey's end; we meet the Greenspans and we learn about the 'game'*

The wheel's squeak-squeak on the tarmac as it landed safely put an end to my maudlin scratchings of the past. As the plane taxied to the terminal, I – full of exhilaration – broke the rules and unfastened my seatbelt, wanting to be among the first batch of disembarkers. Maybe it was that I was gearing up a major smuggling coup or, in all probability, perhaps it was a guilty twinge, as she, *She who Cannot be Ignored*, certainly hadn't been in the forefront of my thoughts. But now, knowing, just knowing, she would be waiting for me at the barrier, I put all inhibitions behind me and, donning my dark glasses, scrambled from the window seat over two of my fellow passengers, eager to be let out, to breathe the air of a new continent. Ignoring the stewardess' glare in retribution for her ignoring my fake smile of apology, I reached the aisle and began to gather my hand luggage from the overhead compartment.

Now disguised as a hybrid between a bag lady and a blind refugee from a duty free store, I entered into an altercation with a man dressed in stripes on his wrist and a plastic visor perched on his eyebrows: "Would you sit down, sir?"

I said: "*Please* ..."

He said: "OK, *please* would you sit down, sir?"

"No ... well, yes," I corrected. "But please, here ..." I gave him some bags to hold as I fished out and presented my specially printed card. It was drawn up by the National Society for the Blind and had the same mantra on it, triplicated in three languages: English, Afrikaans and Tswana. I directed his attention to the English print: *I am blind. Please can you be of assistance?*

He probed deeper: "How can you possibly point out the English if you're blind?"

"Elementary my dear Watson," I said as I groped and grabbed at his shoulder for support. "The English print is embossed, the Afrikaans has a specific odor and the Tswana, nobody can understand it anyway." He sniffed at the card testingly.

"You're right," he grimaced. "Vomit?" And then fate dealt me a blow below the belt. He sneered, "Tell me then, Mister Blind Man, how did you know my name was Watson, huh?" as he jabbed at his chest with his thumb.

True, there it was, pinned to his pectoral, a gold plasticky nametag with black lettering spelling out my immediate problem: CH. STWD. WATSON. What on earth was I supposed to do now? It was all up in the cards. I could probably pretend to throw an epileptic fit or, alternatively, employ some finesse in extracting myself from the bog I was sinking into. Whatever the outcome, I had to keep Chief Steward Watson holding onto my hand luggage – come what may.

"What?" Feigning stupidity. I was playing for time.

"Not 'what' – *WATSON!* You said 'elementary, my dear *WATSON*'."

I was now playing for time in the premier champions league: "No no no, no no ..." It would have been denial *ad infinitum* had he not begun to transfer the bags back into my hands. I had to stop them in transit so I took the bull by the horns. "Ch. Stwd. Dubbleyou, please forgive me. What

I said was: 'ed lamuntri madar wazzon.' It's Tswana for 'I am blind, please can you be of assistance?' I *told* you nobody can understand it anyway."

Now it was in the lap of the Gods.

He was sinking fast and his last instinctive clutch at the straw was very halfhearted indeed. "Yes ... OK ... but ... but how did you guess I was a steward? How?"

"Elementary, my dear Dubbleyou. It's your cologne. I just love your cologne."

He said: "Thank you, sir."

I said: "Can you help me down the steps?"

He presented a bent elbow: "Okilidocally, here, take my arm."

We were off and running.

Hesitantly, arm through arm, down the steps we went and, still attached but radiating more confidence, we traversed the tarmac and passed through the gateway of Afrika with the discreet sign over its portal informing all and sundry that the right of admission was reserved. My Siamese twin whisked me through passport control and stalled at the green light. I increased the pressure on his arm through mine. The weight of the parcels may have started to take their toll and my body language begged him not to abandon me.

"The green light?" he inquired.

"Let's gamble the green," I replied with a wide visually impaired grin. "It's only Hanukkah gifts."

Little did he know that presents for six dependents, times the eight nights of Hanukkah, made ample cause to be arrested as a big-time dreidel smuggler. The spin-off was in the wise rabbinical adage: 'Don't look at the dreidel but rather what is within.' Under all the bubble wrap, inside one of those dreidels was something so valuable it was literally priceless. A score of king's ransoms could never redeem what was now swinging around in a plastic bag in the hands of Dubbleyou. It was still under consideration whether it should be secretly handed over to the Israeli government, but in the meantime it was being put into safekeeping.

I had chosen well. We passed through.

Now I had to rid myself of my appendage. "I'm not really blind, you know," I informed him as I unthreaded the packages from his forearm and strung them on mine. "Could I have my arm back, please?"

"You're horrid, and that's nice," I was informed as he tightened his squeeze on my arm. This was beginning to be a trifle annoying.

"Well the truth is ..." His elbow jabbed my ribs as his bicep pulled me closer in anticipation of the truth. "The truth is ... hey, smile you're on Candid Camera." I pointed over his shoulder and as he spun around to search out the hidden cameras, I extricated my arm and disappeared into the swirling masses.

Had it been intuition? Perhaps not. But there she was at the barrier, standing where Costas should have been. "Hi Hon. Kiss-kiss. I haven't forgotten the presents."

It would be nice to be made to feel welcome after such a long absence.

"Kiss-kiss. Presents shmesents. How was your flight? Listen up, Hon, Costas is very sick. I think he's going to die."

"The flight? Fine, I got someone to shlep the bags and don't Hon me, Hon. With Costas sick, what about Hanukkah celebrations? I'll be stuck with eighty-four dreidels."

"That's forty-eight, Poophead."

"I love you too. So call me a small time dreidel smuggler."

That is what first attracted me to her. It was the sharpness of her most extraordinary of minds. We had reached out to each other, our karmas crashing. In the wake of our telepathic collision, as we braced for the impact's shock wave, we had our first misunderstanding and I told her my first lie.

She said, "Shrapnelle."

I said, "Ye-bigtime."

She said, "Bigtime shmigtime, Shrapnelle is my name – Dumbo."

"Dumbo shmumbo, pleased to meet you," I flirted back. "I'm Camouflage." That was the lie.

It wasn't that we were led by each other's individual imagination, it was more an intertwining of our visceral essences and she holds me in her power as I hold her in mine. I also have the utmost of respect for her mule kick. A combination of balance, power and speed, with a healthy dash of Chi thrown in for good measure, renders it invisible. It blitzes up out of nowhere and the strobe flash in the center of the head, as the consciousness hitchhikes a lift with the exploding light waves on their never ending journey to the outreaches of oblivion, has some horrible side effects.

Once, on arriving home sapped from my day's activities, I made a concerted effort to be amenable: "Hi Hon – I'm ho-ome! Did anybody get round to doing some food shopping today?" My cheery query was not received ecstatically and the sequences of events were as follows:

First, she growled like a pit bull.

Then, flaring her lips and, with a collection of half a dozen or so short staccato hisses, she inhaled through gritted teeth. Adrenalin propelled her from her prone position on the sofa as she, jaws still clenched, exhaled, her lips vibrating in resonance with her "OK OK OK OK OK ..."

"Please stop gnashing, Hon." The 'please' was an attempt to restore her equilibrium. A tranquilizer dart would have been better.

"So – what do you want?" She glared as she auditioned for a junior tympani percussion band. It sounded as if the industrial revolution had finally made an appearance as she thrashed those pots and their lids around the kitchen sink.

"Anything. Just anything your little heart desires, Hon." In retrospect I don't think I should have said that, but it just popped out. As she rehearsed her cymbal solo, I distanced myself. Working at the far end of the counter top, I rustled up a quick sandwich and got the coffee underway.

Then two things coincided; I swallowed the last of my sandwich and she slammed what she had concocted down in front of me.

"Here! Wait till you're finished eating before you drink your coffee!"

"You command and I obey, Hon, but I'll take my coffee now if you don't mind. I'm not hungry anymore."

POW!

That night, I went to bed hungry.

We left the terminal in the direction of home, both of us subdued with the thought of Costas dying so soon after DuBois' accident. "I have to make one stop on the way." I yawned, sapped from the trip. "And do you think you can drive with both hands on the wheel, please?"

"Do you think you can cover your mouth when you yawn?" she countered. "It's *mikve* night (ritual immersion before knowing one's partner) tonight and I don't want to fight, so please, do not tell me how to drive. OK?"

"Okilidocally, Hon," I bounced back.

"Okilidocally? Where did you hear that from?"

"Just trying to be lovey, Hon ... just trying to be lovey."

"Where's our stop? The RPG?" she asked and answered with a querying glance in my direction.

"Yes, the RPG and do you think you can keep your eyes on the road? Take the next left if you don't mind, I think it's quicker."

Ignoring my navigational prompting she carried straight on. Every cloud has a silver lining – at least she was throttling the steering wheel with both hands and not some part of me. I always sat in the back seat when she drove. To all intents and purposes it only gave an illusion of safety but as her silver lining was stamped with the hallmark of death I took a *ta'anit dibur* (self imposed vow of silence) as a safety measure and was grateful that fate had positioned me out of striking distance.

A *ta'nit dibur* is a terribly powerful weapon and, if skilfully implemented, can drive a life partner mad. But against Shrapnelle an arsenal of powder puffs would have made more sense as she counterattacked by turning to telepathy. She cocked her eye at me in the rear view mirror and I cocked my eye back at her. A rather cheeky thing to do under the circumstances but, as we looked at each other cock-eyed, she socked me psychically and her thoughts became part of my consciousness: "You've just blown it Buddy Boy – no *mikve* tonight."

Whammo! My head snapped back against the backrest. She had won on a technical knockout. I left my head against the backrest, my ego accepting defeat and let my mind pick up its *wandelstok* and head on out. Blessed with a short attention span, I could never be bored with my mind's wonderings. With the imagery of constantly changing venues ever-presenting new vistas, I reencountered my first confrontation with the RPG.

Rabbi Pinchas Greenspan, or as he was better known, the RPG, together with the *Rebitzin* Buncker, who packed a *kugel* on the *platta* hot plate and a strudel or two as a backup in the freezer, were my beloved parents-in-law. I had married into a Hassidic dynasty, which was no mean feat for a practicing Litvisher. I had proved my mettle by showing I could hold my liquor as well as the next man. Swallowing Bronfyn together with my pride had endeared me to them.

I remember our initial meeting as if it was yesterday. In retrospect, if I had taken Costas' advice more seriously –

"Put your brain into gear before you put your mouth into motion" – it certainly would have made for plainer sailing. Just as my initial meeting with Shrapnelle had begun with *hashgaha elyona* (divine intervention) – and deteriorated into a misunderstanding, so it was with the RPG. But, be that as it may, it was the first time I was proclaimed an *Apicorus* (Epicurean) by a halahic authority.

I had awoken with trepidation that particular Friday. Would the bag of tricks I'd picked up at Upholder's School hold me in good stead? If I'd known that fate, after bottom dealing me so many dead man's hands, would deliver aces, I wouldn't have been repeatedly muttering to myself "So much to do and so little time"; fretting that I had too few hours left before candle lightening time, which signifies the onset of the Shabbat. And I still had to iron my white shirt.

I'd been invited to participate in the RPG's Friday night meal where I anticipated a formal inquiry characteristic of a grilling interrogation into my past, present and future plans. The jewel in the crown of the evening's entertainment would be the prospective's obligatory *dvar Torah* (teaching from the Torah). Irrespective of what fate intended, as my hole card in the game of poker *pilpul* (hair-splitting hermeneutics) to be played around the gefilte fish that evening, I had the ace of diamonds, the jewel from the crown, as an insurance policy. Slipped up my sleeve I had a *hidush* (original teaching).

"I have two questions." The RPG's eyes stopped reflecting the spiritual holiness of Shabbat and took on the black hardness of the nose end of a double-barreled shotgun. "Potential sons-in-law fall into two categories; those who consider themselves considerable know-it-alls and those who rate themselves as total ignoramuses. Into which category do you fall?"

He discharged the second barrel: "What is further, from East to West or from down to up?"

As he leant back into his chair to reload, a cold hand clutched at my heart. Having come armed only with genial honesty, I was in truth experiencing the divine intervention of *hashgaha elyona*; or was I being set up? For I had the answers to both questions. I had been dealt a pair of aces. So as not to squander them, careful game play was called for. I reckoned I would bluff with my first ace; hum and haw, fumble and fake and – whammo, slap it down on the pure white Shabbat tablecloth, together with its partner and the two right answers, and enjoy my chicken soup before it got too cold.

"*Nu*?"

His *nu* of impatience broke the spell and I covered up the involuntary jerk that accompanied my return to real time by reaching for the salt. Clumsy me. I had inadvertently brushed against a wine goblet with the cuff of my shirt and, as the red wine flowed across the white tablecloth, I oversalted the soup, trying my best to disassociate myself from the spreading Rorschach stain, the blood of my self sacrifice.

*Rebitzin* Bunker whimsically saved me from additional embarrassment: "It's a *s'gula* (charm/talisman)," she sighed, "for the wedding night." Her cheeks took on the hue of the ruined tablecloth.

"Soup not salty enough for you?" The Rabbi pointed with his first two fingers at the crimson cloth. "Shake some salt onto that sabbatical skid mark. Now, I still have to hear what you have to say for yourself, young man. Maybe stop humming and hawing? Your soup's getting cold."

Now was the appropriate time to play my ace of hearts. For the sake of accuracy and to give credit when credit is due, it was the GWEQ of BP's adamancy which provided me with the answer to the first question.

When I was a youngster, a very popular bar mitzvah present was a book voucher for the C.N.A. store. My peers and cohorts would cash theirs in for an annual subscription to *The Beano* or *The Boys World Magazine*; but for me? It was a no-no; *Verboten*. It would have been delivered weekly and somewhere inside would be another episode of 'the game'.

Oh, how I'd yearned for an annual subscription to that magazine. *The Boys World Magazine* invariably included a page, entitled: WHAT WOULD *YOU* DO? It portrayed a healthy looking lad, a prime specimen of youth, for the young reader to emulate and identify with, in a dire, life-threatening situation. One example was a picture of two pals who'd gone hiking through a swamp. One of them had stepped into quicksand. He was sucked in up to his chest and the only thing keeping his head above the sand's swampy surface was his hiking partner, who was pulling on his outstretched arm.

Another illustration had a man in the frozen north surrounded by a pack of hungry wolves. He had a gun but he'd run short of ammunition; he was down to his last bullet.

When I was still in Upholder School, once a week Costas and DuBois would set me a homework project on providing solutions to the predicaments depicted on the WHAT WOULD *YOU* DO? page. After considering all the possibilities, we would vote on the best of the suggestions.

After smuggling the contraband publication into the house, I would lock myself in the toilet, as one had to study the page carefully. Every object illustrated could be utilized in extracting the doomed unfortunates. This was part of the fun. Suspecting the worst, the GWEQ of BP would authoritatively ratatattat on the lavatory door, insisting on knowing either what was going on or what was I doing inside there for such a long time. When I yelled back "homework", I think she probably went into a state of temporary shock, both at the choice of location and also at the occurrence of such an erratic phenomenon, for she would leave me in peace for at least another ten minutes or so before attempting another assault on my privacy.

The magazine's publishers, for some unfathomable reason, possibly as a disservice to its readers, would print the wrong answer to the game on the second to last page. Any unsuspecting reader who perchance found himself sinking in a swamp of quicksand would be badly done by if he followed the publisher's advice. Cutting a piece of swamp-side bamboo and improvising a snorkel, while a friend ran for help, would have disastrous ramifications. Bamboo is not as hollow as *The Boys World Magazine* would like us to believe.

The escape from death the triumvirate finally voted in as being the most suitable retained a brutal simplicity even though it was twofold: jerk your buddy into the quicksand and clamber over his body onto terra firma, then, after cutting your friend a piece of bamboo, so *he* can go snorkeling, rush off to assemble a rescue party. Why? What would you do?

To this day I still play the WHAT WOULD *YOU* DO? game as an amusing interlude to life. I imagine myself in a life-threatening situation and I conjure up ways of saving myself. The additional allure being that I could play at G*d. If a plan didn't pan out as suspected, I could revert and choose a different alley up which to proceed until, after numerous attempts, I would extricate myself. When I'm feeling low, I'd sometimes rather choose a spectacular death for myself and instead of glorifying myself as a self-savior, I would attend my own funerals. There was always a sad turnout to those functions.

Naturally the GWEQ of BP would insist she escort me all the way to the North End Branch of the C.N.A. bookstore to make quite sure I didn't fritter my book vouchers away on anything inappropriate and rather invested my finances in something suitable that would stand me in good stead for the future. No amount of pleading or peer pressure (e.g. but so-and-so's mother lets him ...) would budge her in the slightest. Billy Bunter was out and the *Chambers's Twentieth Century Dictionary* together with the *Complete Works of Oscar Wilde* was in. It took me four years before I eventually got over her imposition.

At seventeen I rediscovered the late Oscar Wilde. The dust jacket had faded but the print inside was most definitely readable. While my school mates at the Stalag were slogging through the likes of *How Green Was My Valley*, there I was, lapping up *The Importance of Being Earnest* as required reading for a paper I was preparing for Upholder School on the subject of lying. Earnest had been presented a poser, similar to the RPG's, by his prospective mother-in-law and it was the subject of the paper to propose different answers for Earnest and to surmise how these alternative replies could have affected the eventual outcome of the story.

While we are giving credit where credit is due, I do have to admit I had more than one reply for the RPG regarding my intelligence. I selected my third option.

"Holy Rabbi, we know there is no limit and no cure for man's stupidity. No matter how many drops of homeopathic medicine one doses oneself with, it will not add one drop of power to the human brain. Take reflexology – *mae'le* (untranslatable), if they would only apply pressure to the head – this I can understand. But to press the feet and expect that to improve the head – how could this be?

"There are *types* who go so far as to apply magnets to their heads. You may find this amusing but you should know that modern technology has enabled us, with the aid of magnets, to remove the stone buildup in washing machines. But I ask of you, *Rebono Shel Olam* (Lord of the Universe), how, after the magnets have quarried out space in the head, can those same magnets fill the evacuated areas with gray matter?"

"*Nu.* So you tell me." The Rabbi was immersed in resalting the wound.

"We are stupid but we are also made in the image of G*d. What can we learn from this?" I was treading on thin ice.

"*Nu?*"

"Holy Rabbi, in reply to your first question I can only unequivocally state that I am divinely stupid."

"With this, I can only agree. What about question number two?"

Umpteen years ago the Greeks had asked the same question and it was not new to me. Somewhere in my memory banks lay the answer. I thanked Costas for his cornering me when no escape hole had opportunely presented itself and, together, our reconstructing a mini Athens in quality and style of debate. He had debated me on this very question number two.

"Science teaches us that the closer a source of light the stronger are its rays. At sunup and sundown we can look into the sun in the east and the west but when the orb is high in the firmament, its rays dazzle if we glance in its direction. Ergo down to up, with its stronger rays, is closer than east to west."

*Rebitzin* Bunker gonged me out with her fork against the cut glass wine decanter.

What? Wrong answer. Well, it seems my bullet had missed its mark.

"What are you, a Hellenist or something?"

Then it dawned. That Cypriot café owner had provided me with a Greek answer. The Holy Rabbi was obviously looking for something more Jewish in nature.

"*Nu.* So are you a hedonist as well or just a plain garden variety Hellenist?"

The *Rebitzen* saved me from answering when she intervened on my behalf: "It was close enough. Wasn't it my dear?"

It was my turn to intervene on the Rabbi's behalf. Armed with geniality, I was prepared to enter the fray. "*Rebitzen,* I appreciate that you want to save the day but there is really no need for you to intercede in order to save me from embarrassment. If Bilaam the Wicked could accept admonishment from a donkey, who am I, not to be admonished by the Great Holy Rabbi?"

Now that – that was the misunderstanding. I've had worse but it was pretty bad.

The Rabbi half rose and brought the palm of his hand down with a slap, right in the middle of a soggy half absorbed briny swamp of wine – Splat! I thought it was *t'hiyat hameitim* (revival of the dead) when the herring jumped off the table. He vibrated a salted finger at me and then it came upon us: "APIKORAS! (heinous apostate!)"

"I don't think he meant it," *Rebitzen* Bunker said to both of us. "Here. Have some gefilte."

She placed it at my setting, a round white ball of gefilte fish half submerged in a pond of gel.

"Here. Have some *Yiddishkeit* (Jewishness)." The Rabbi piled on three healthy dollops of white orthodox *chrein* (horseradish). It still floated. The disc of carrot, balanced on top, was in all probability a flotation device preventing it from being totally enveloped into the half solid goop.

This was the final test. If I could ingest what was in front of me it would give credence to my *bona fides* and establish beyond doubt that I was who I said I was.

I lapped it up and, forgetting my manners, mopped the *she'rayim* (leftover residue) with a chunk of *halla* (Shabbat bread).

The *Rebitzin* announced, "Welcome to the family darling." She glowed with pleasure that I had so easily made myself at home. "We all loved you from the beginning. Yes, including the Rabbi. Could you believe he fed the last boy the head from the gefilte?"

We each had a piece of chicken and dessert was served.

It was in all probability a hypnogogic illusion but I could have sworn a fanfare of trumpets heralded the arrival of the *pièce de résistance* – Mother's Trifle.

"*Nu,* do you have anything else you'd like to tell us?" The Rabbi picked up his dessert spoon and used it as a baton, providing a tempo to my hesitation; my swansong. "Or should we eat dessert and *bensch* (say grace after meals)?" It would have been churlish of me to pass over his broad hint that the eleventh hour was upon us and it was *dvar Torah* time.

"Holy Rabbi, I have a *hiddush.*"

"So you have a *hiddush,* some new wisdom? *Nu,* would you like to share it?" He began polishing his spoon with the *halla dekel* (fabric bread-cover) in anticipation.

"Holy Rabbi, we are taught that every commandment we fulfill from the Torah brings us closer to the final redemption. But I believe there is one specific commandment that, when fulfilled, especially speeds up the arrival of Messiah son of David."

"He should come quickly in our time."

Following the RPG'S directive to get on with it, I got on with it. "We read in this week's Torah portion that we are obligated to help one's fellow man load up his donkey. Tradition also teaches us that the Messiah will arrive mounted on a donkey. So when I helped Mrs Gimpel with her shopping to her car, in addition to helping her load up the donkey as we are commanded, I, on a different level, was loading up the universal donkey of redemption. Together with Mrs Gimpel's groceries I was giving the Messiah a leg up into the saddle. He should come quickly in our time."

The Rabbi was slow in coming to a decision "*Nu.* That's all? What is this? It's deep." He reflectively probed with his spoon into the depths of his dessert.

The good *Rebitzen* Bunker decided for him: "It's Mother's Trifle. You love Mother's Trifle. We have it every week."

"Really? I've never eaten anything like this before." The Rabbi reinvestigated with his spoon. "I couldn't possibly have any of this anyway; I'm too full, thank you very much. I suggest that perhaps we should all, instead, have a *lechai'im* (shot of vodka).

"What do you all say?"

"Oyveir ve 'boleil'," (bottoms up).

## I play the game

The squeal of complaining Goodyear retreads, as the asphalt took a healthy bite out of their rubber, in conjunction with a threatened whiplash, as Shrapnelle pulled over, was a wonderful reintroduction to reality. Worse was yet to come.

"End of the line for you, buster. Come on – get out, we're blocking traffic."

"What do you mean?" I was ratty at being woken up so unceremoniously and had good reason to sulk. "You should have turned left when I told you. Now I have to walk two blocks to the RPG's. My way was better."

"Not if you're going to the mall."

"The mall? Now? What for?"

"To buy Hanukah gifts"

"But ..."

"I tell you this every year. Please try and get it through that thick skull of yours: nobody plays with dreidels anymore!"

At least now I had a deeper understanding of her antagonism towards me. I had slipped up once again. It was all put down to my chronic inadequacy as a shopper.

"I'm sorry I'm lacking ..." I half mumbled to myself. Not

brave enough to voice it out loud, I let my apology peter out.

But she had picked up on it. "I'm not interested in hearing an apology. All I'm interested in is hearing you say it won't happen again."

"OK. It won't happen again."

"Yeah – Yeah – Yeah. Now out you get, and please try to remember not to slam the door ... and don't forget the dreidels."

"Oopsadaisy, nearly forgot." I was halfway out and as I leant back across the backseat to retrieve the precious bag of dreidels, I surreptitiously extracted a bottle of duty free whiskey from the clutter of packages lying on the floor.

But it was to no avail. I forget, she can see through lead. "Don't. Just don't you and the RPG get drunk again ..."

Whiskey can give a man courage.

SLAM went the car door.

SCREEEECH went the tires and, as I jumped smartly out the way to save my toes from being run over by the fishtailing backend, she sped off.

Under normal circumstances having to walk two blocks would be only a hop, skip and a jump, but jet lag had reduced my normal sprightly stride into a shuffle, skip and a scuffle. The skip was over any cracks in the sidewalk. Why go looking for trouble? For the geniuses who abound, the periodic skip in my gait would be diagnosed as a Tourette twitch. For the other three percent of the population, who modestly did not consider themselves know-it-alls, I would just be another one of them; a poor, red-eyed lunatic. My disguise was perfect.

My skips down the sidewalk, in association with their destination, struck a chord. I had often played *The Boys World Magazine* game with the RPG's story. I had a block and a half left to go, so there was enough time for the abridged version:

WHAT WOULD *YOU* DO? Russian Style, 1919.

"You are the mother-lode of all evil; a practitioner of foul superstition. The tail of the Devil, those strings you whisper incantations to and court with kisses are part and parcel of your loathsome depravity. But the vilest of acts, the infliction of your repugnant ritual dabbling, be it even on the frogspawn of Jewish whores, cannot and will not be tolerated by society. In accordance, you, you despicable Jew, are sentenced to ..." He glanced at the prosecutor who signaled with four fingers. "Four? That's three for me is it?" The prosecutor acquiesced with a nod; quite happy with his one thousand ruble share of the bribe: "So you, you Hassidic rat, you are sentenced to a class B conviction; effective immediately."

Pinhas Greenspan, a young anemic *mohel* (ritual circumciser), had just been committed to a Siberian work camp for twelve years. The four thousand ruble bribe, scraped up by the community, had prolonged his existence for as little as six months – the expected lifespan of a professionless Jew in the Siberian Tundra. The Honorable Justice could have shown an iota of humanitarian feeling by passing a quick, merciful death sentence.

"Rancid Jew, tell us all. Do you have anything to say before your loathsome presence is finally removed from this courtroom?"

The hapless, introverted Pinhas Greenspan, the promising halahic scholar and itinerant ritual circumciser, who had never spoken a public word in his life, surprised even himself when he took the Honorable Justice up on his offer.

He raised his thumb and curved it through the air in a climbing half circle. His habitual *swish*, picked up in the yeshiva world, ended with his thumb at its crescent, breaking the line of sight connecting the Honorable Justice and himself. As they both focused on the extended digit, Pinhas Greenspan, the doomed Jew, had his day in court.

"*Ein yiush ba'olam* (there is no despair in this world)," he declared.

That was not all; there was more to come. They both lost track of the thumb; the Honorable Justice, when his convict began bouncing, leaping higher and higher, Pinhas Greenspan, when he, his ritual fringes fluttering in the updraft, was overcome with ecstasy and his eyes rolling up into the back of his head.

With knees jerking up to meet his chest at the crest of each accumulating spring, he broke out in joyous song "*Mitzvah gedola leh'yot be'simha tamid.*" Proclaiming it is G*d's given commandment to be continually in a state of joy.

Not even the Honorable Justice's howl – "Remove the mad Jew!" – could stop his elevated jiggering. Pinhas Greenspan bounced out of court as if it was the happiest day of his life.

Who would have hazarded the thought or had an inkling of a notion: even the most gullible swallowers of incredulous stories would never have believed that, within two years and two whole months, Pinhas Greenspan would once more pass through the portals of that very same court building – but this time as a free man?

After five days interspaced with thorough beatings, when his lone travel companion and fellow prisoner felt sober enough to administer them, Pinhas Greenspan decided the time had come to stop being in a continual state of joy and to take stock of his situation. He sat on the small wooden crate which had held all his belongings, until the *Yok* had traded his hard-boiled eggs through the slats in their railway car to some wayside peasants. All forty eight of them, a contribution from the community – one from each family's Seder plate – used in the ritualistic Passover feast celebrating freedom – in exchange for seven bottles of vodka. Three of the bottles were already empty. Time was running out for Pinhas Greenspan. He sat on the crate, holding what was left of his matzo, and took stock.

Besides his name, the clothes he was wearing, the one blanket that each prisoner was allowed, together with what was left of his provisions, which were to have lasted a journey of at least three weeks, all of Pinhas Greenspan's worldly assets constituted a horseradish root, which he had hidden from the *Yok* in his cap, a present from his mother, and conflicting advice from his parents.

His father's parting words, that he commands his son to live and no matter what would come to be, his survival was the most important thing, together with his mother's instruction that death is not the end and he should cut his wrists with the circumcision knife, her present to him which she had sewed into the hem of his ritual fringe garment, if he was forced to eat the *dvar aher* (pig), left him confused.

Except for the snow that drifted in through the slats as the transport train metronomically clack clack-clack clacked its way inexorably through the frozen semi tundra onwards toward the leaden horizon to its destination of doom you have the full picture.

Now, WHAT WOULD *YOU* DO?

Don't make the error of disregarding the *Yok*, as he is an integral player in the game.

He invariably introduced himself as Nikolai Shaygitzovitz, an appropriate name for a true-blooded White Russian, "From the town of Sheisstoyk. Master Sandpaper Manufacturer."

He was a gruesome man when sober and his family condoned his alcoholism, sometimes promoting it, as long as it didn't hamper the efficient daily running of the family business. His wife oversaw the business from her workbench on the factory floor and was quite happy with this arrangement. She was the driving force behind Russia's biggest sandpaper factory. She had inherited it as a struggling enterprise when her father-in-law, a gruesome man when sober, had fainted into a vat of bubbling hide glue. She had sweated day and night for years to establish a vibrant concern which, when in its heyday, would eventually trade as far afield as Springfield, America.

Proud of its town of origin, the product was merchandised as *Sheispaper*. The name soon became a popular household byword for anything Russian that was of a good rough quality.

He was a garrulous drunk and most of his working hours were spent drinking in his office, talking to himself. It was a bottle of imported slivovitz that lead to his downfall. Ironically he was gruesomely sober when he smashed the bottle over the tax collector's head.

Perhaps the tax collector had been overly diligent in arriving early for his monthly bribe, since, as he was shown in, his taxpayer was struggling with the cork from the bottle. This all came out in court. The collector admitted to having in the past enjoyed accepting the taxpayer's libatious offerings, but never before, or as a substitute for, breakfast.

He, however, flatly denied ever suggesting he would be open to accepting an *unopened*, imported bottle of slivovitz in lieu of bribe. Nikolai Shaygitzovitz was sentenced to two years.

As was his way, he had introduced himself to his new world, which had a population of two and the perimeters of a cattle car.

"I am Nikolai Shaygitzovitz from the town of Sheisstoyk. Master Sandpaper Manufacturer and miserable specimen of humanity. I have lost it all – my wife, my honor. I have been brought down. But you, Jew, you give me hope, for when I see you before me I don't feel so degraded or badly injured after all. You lowly spawn of Satan Himself – you cheer me considerably. Come, I will tell you all. Come and drink with me!"

Who would turn down such an offer; look such a gift

horse in the mouth? Pinhas Greenspan could and did. It was Passover and for its duration, following his mother's sound advice, he felt he would rather slit his veins than let any *hameitz* (leaven) pass his lips. One could feel some empathy for Pharaoh and the Egyptians if any *one* of the Plagues were as intensive as the thrashing Pinhas Greenspan received at the hand of the insulted, not yet drunk, Nikolai Shaygitzovitz.

Pinhas Greenspan sat on his crate and focused on the three remaining bottles of vodka, realizing that when they were finished so was he. There was no escape. The sliding door to the cattle truck would only be opened at its destination. He closed his eyes to shut out the mocking bottled elixir that remained of his life and began to think.

He thought.

He took stock of his situation and thought for a long time. He smiled, opened his eyes and spoke.

"Master Shaygitz ..." he used the diminutive form of the name. "Master Shaygitz, please tell me about sandpaper."

Nikolai Shaygitzovitz needed no better invitation. He spoke about paper; he spoke about glue; he spoke about grinding glass. He spoke until he passed out. When he awoke, it was not long before he was once again elixired. It didn't take much to gear him up.

"Master Shaygitz, what in your opinion is the best way to make hide glue?"

"Now the most important thing about hide glue is ..."

He spoke and he spoke and he spoke while Pinhas Greenspan listened and listened and listened.

The weather changed as they trundled northwards – clack clack-clack clack, "... care must be taken, when melting the sand, the ..." clack clack-clack clack, "... cover your face with a wet woolen rag so that you don't breathe ..." clack clack-clack clack, "... when sorting the sheets ..."

Clickety-clack. The calendar and the latitude turned long nights into shivering seminars in sandpapering; and as the coldness increased, so did the intake of vodka that ignited a cozy blaze in the belly. Graduation day was close at hand; there remained less than half a bottle.

"Master Shaygitz, I take my hat off to you, for you have taught me all there is to know about sandpaper." Pinhas Greenspan doffed his cap and out tumbled the horseradish onto Nikolai Shaygitzovitz's lap. Oops.

Some say it was the 30-30-30 factor that saved Pinhas Greenspan's life, others put it down to alcoholism, but I surmise it was that root of horseradish he'd kept hidden from the Goy which ultimately was his saving grace. (Perhaps, as I myself have an affinity to the root. The smallest of nibbles begs for a shot of Bronfyn to extinguish the inferno spreading through one's innards. It raises the body temperature until it feels like the fire of the dragon when one exhales through the nose. This is why the Yoks call it Dragonroot.)

"Why! Damn you to hell, you slithering worker of the Devil, Jew. What, from the blue blazes of hell, have you conjured up in your cap? You bastard from Satan's semen – it's Dragonroot, and a goodly piece at that. Pass that vodka you mongrel of mankind!"

He had already started gnawing at the root when Pinhas Greenspan handed him the remaining half bottle.

"Master, how is the Dragonroot? Perhaps later I will take you up on your offer of a drink?"

His Master drank and gauged the level of the bottle critically.

"You know, my dear Jew, some people look and they see a half empty cup, while others see a cup that is half full. As for myself, my dear Jew, what is it to me, as I drink straight from the bottle? And as for you; if you so much as think of asking for a drink again you will fall foul of me. I will smash this bottle, together with whatever is left in it, over your cranium, you aborted drop of a whore, you stagnant issue."

Pinhas Greenspan retired to his crate and slowly gauged the ever-diminishing level of the bottle as Nikolai Shaygitzovitz munched away on the horseradish.

"I'm a firebrand! I'm burning up! What have you fed me, Jew? Help your Master off with his coat before I strangle you, wring your scrawny neck with your own sidelocks."

Pinhas Greenspan helped his Master shuck off his fleece-lined coat.

"Drink, Master, drink. It will put out the fire. Here, let me help you unbutton your shirt. It will cool you down."

"I have a dragon in my belly. I breathe fire."

"Drink, Master, drink. It will put out the fire. Here, let me fan you with your shirt."

Pinhas Greenspan peeled the shirt off the heavily perspiring torso and began to flap it vigorously. His Master was indeed suffering. The road map of broken blood vessels that normally webbed his face was washed away by a borscht-red flood of lava-hot dragon breath that radiated from under his skin. Pinhas Greenspan was thunderstruck by the rivers of perspiration that reflected the tinge of the skin. Or was he really sweating blood?

"Here, Master, let me help you get naked ..." He began pulling off his master's boots. "... So you can cool off in the wind through the slats."

"I will drink to your sound advice, Jew."

"Thank you, Master, it will put out the fire."

As the naked Nikolai Shaygitzovitz lurched to his feet, his hot blood rushed to his head and flooded his consciousness. He passed out. Pinhas Greenspan left him there, sprawled where he'd collapsed, on the cattle truck floor. He leaned over and retrieved the dropped bottle. Peering through the slats he saw the gloom of late afternoon had been dyed black by the darkness of night. The eighth and final day of Passover was over. There remained enough vodka for one good drink.

"Here's to cutting it fine." He raised the bottle and toasted his horizontal master: *"Hamavdil bein kodesh lehol."* The bottle was empty. *"Lecha'im."*

The icy Tundra winds that blew in through the slats cooled Nikolai Shaygitzovitz down all right. By morning he had frozen to death.

That, in a nutshell is the RPG's story. There remain two unanswered questions: What is the 30-30-30 factor and how did Pinhas Greenspan account for his actions when the cattle car's doors were slid open at its destination? I had arrived at *my* destination, the RPG's building, and if my timing isn't off I could wind up his story in the elevator ride up to the forth level. Each level up, the lower or deeper into the depths of depravity reached the deeds.

Level one — the first and least loathsome of all. Pinhas Greenspan exchanged his coat and boots with those of a corpse. G*d forgive him.

Level two — Pinhas Greenspan unripped his mother's stitching and, with tears rolling down his cheeks, cut off his sidelocks and trimmed his beard to a stubble with his circumcision knife. G*d forgive him.

Level three took seven seconds in the elevator but in real life it took five days — Nikolai Shaygitzovitz slightly defrosted during the day. The wind and the nightly refreezing had preserved him in a state of frosty ossification. There was no bleeding when on the fifth day Pinhas Greenspan finally took up courage and his circumcision knife once again, and cut the Yok down to size. No forgiveness is needed from G*d, for without G*d having guided his hand he would not have been able to do it. There was to be no doubt as to who he was.

Level four — the timing was spot on; we had reached our destiny.

"PRISONERS OUT!"

*"Ping!"* As the elevator doors slid open, so did the sliding doors of the cattle truck. Into a new world he

stepped, right into a puddle, and announced: "I am Nikolai Shaygitzovitz from the town of Sheisstoyk. Master Sandpaper Manufacturer. The Jew is dead."

The janitor mopping the landing floor must have thought I was mad.

I skidded past him with a hurried nod and rang the RPG's bell.

"*Nu!* Come in, come in. I've been waiting breathlessly for you. Do you have it?"

"Here, take the whole bag. Nobody plays with dreidels anymore."

At minus thirty degrees in a wind of thirty miles per hour it takes a naked man thirty seconds to freeze to death. This is the 30-30-30 wind factor.

**A poignant tale of love**
***I follow the RPG's instructions and I plan a jailbreak.***

The next morning I told my wife that, in my eyes, she was the most exquisite of gems and I could never sully her with presents of inferior diamonds; she told me to eff off.

That was where the manuscript ran out of pages. I got up and stretched. On reflection it seemed to me a higgledy-piggledy hodgepodge of a story. But, on the other hand, parts of it were missing.

I sat down to reread it and forge a plan of action. Inside of me a germ of an idea was conceived, its cells, seething in a pattern of geometrical gestation, would soon develop into a full-blown virus, waiting to be born into the world of self survival.

The only thing I was really sure of at this stage of the game was I was no longer looking for Quentin Locke, the author of the manuscript. Of course Stephen didn't have to know this; he was to be kept in the dark about my sights now being set on higher gains.

My new target was something much smaller; something that could be hidden inside a dreidel perhaps, if needs be, *if* it existed at all. Not much to go by at first glance, I must admit. But I still had untapped resources. The time had come to prepare myself for a search on the psychic web.

I fished out my old textbook: *Endeavors in Psychic Practice.*

It was written so long ago, parts of it didn't mean much anymore. As with most textbooks of that era, it is frustratingly wishy-washy in its specifics, is generally written in the third person and sometimes is inclined to wander off into the fourth or fifth. Careful reading is prescribed if one is to glean anything at all. The feats of yesteryear, accomplishments once heralded as psychic conquests, now seemed in retrospect to be nothing more than amusing idiosyncratic demonstrations of unconventional behavior. But some parts are still highly pertinent:

*Practitioners of symbiotic telepathic communication should be made aware of the inherent danger of this activity. The symbiotic character of the undertaking involves the entry of the person's mind into that of the telepathic partner, and in a process of reversal – the telepathic partner's mind takes up residence in that of the first person's. The inherent danger, which of late has become to be known as the* Absentminded Syndrome*, is first whimsically described as the process wherein one telepathic partner* absentmindedly *forgets part of his mind when it vacates its temporary premises and so complicates his partner's own retrieval, due to the fact that necessary occupancy space has been taken up by portions of mislaid mind.*

*And, indeed, it is not so whimsical in the least, when this is done premeditatedly by the rogue telepathist, who intentionally deposits unwanted parts of his mind, and so traps valuable, but now* homeless *portions of others' minds which cannot return to their landlords as there is now inadequate space for them at their home base – so producing a feeling of absentmindedness in the party. The elderly are the easy victims of this mind piracy. The neophyte must appreciate the dangers involved.*

*The necessary basis for any successful attempt in psychic*

*communication depends entirely on an intrinsic predisposition. After the aptitude has been discovered, the fundamental capacity can be enhanced with a deeper appreciation of technique, which is unfortunately inexplicable and, at best, can only be comprehended in allegory. Telepathy is akin to occult magic, but goes two steps beyond.*

*The primary exercise at hand is to station oneself opposite a wall-clock, taking up a distance of at least a half dozen paces. While looking at the dial, call up a facial image of a person, with its likeness suspended in front of the clock. This mental projection is* transparent *and does not obstruct the face of the clock.*

*Train yourself to focus on the hanging image until you find that simultaneously focusing on both the clock and the imagined image is impossible. While focusing on the image, the mind prevents you from reading the clock, since it is engaged in focusing on something that does not exist. Now in reverse; attempt to focus on the clock without losing sight of the imaginary face; still being aware of it in your peripheral vision. This is what you are aiming for. The practitioners of the occult use this ethereal projection in an attempt to impose their influences. Mastery of this application is easily grasped.*

*It is the secondary stage that can present difficulty, and some find it beyond their grasp, but with perseverance it can be accomplished. This stage, one step beyond the occult, may take time and considerable effort.*

*The transparent, or semi transparent image, must now be* filled in *with your mind so that the projection takes on a more solid form and it indeed blocks out the view of the clock entirely. Can you walk around the image and see its back quarters? Does the image have a reflection in the mirror? Would it sneeze if you tickled its nose with a feather?*

*The tertiary, or final, stage is the final step into the beyond. It, as described above, encompasses the interchanging of minds with the telepathic partner. This can only be done with the partner's participation and his simultaneous interchange of minds with an image of yours (that* image of yours *is the fifth person) that he has made up in his mind's eye.*

*How is this done? It can only be realized by an* adept *or* sensitive.

I perched on the side of the bed and composed myself in the Ottoman mirror above my ex's vanity table. I mused at the irony in the myriad of unclaimed scents and colognes, abandoned colours that cluttered the base of the arched mirror and were multiplied in the looking glass's depth; an ocular step through a doorway, shaped like half of the Ten Commandments. (Thou shalt not covet, bear false witness, commit adultery, steal ... that includes your husband's love ... etc.) A doorway that reflected the world of forsaken adoration. Ah, all the perfumes of Arabia.

Looking deeply within, I launched my mind like a kite into the psychic-sphere. The string of consciousness it was tugging on would act as an antenna. If Mr Quentin Locke was out there, we would cross lines and our kites would swoop in high unison, wafting in the hot updraft of telepathic communication. I felt a vibration. Then I noticed his reflection in the mirror. He was kneeling on the bed behind me, peering over my shoulder. How long had he been there?

*"I have always been with you,"* he answered. *"Scoot on over."*

I scooted over, making room for him, and we looked at each other in the mirror. All four of us. Me, with his reflection and he with mine, like musketeers – a quadroconscious being – all for one and one for all.

# CHAPTER SIX

I phoned Stephen and hit him with it. "I've found him."

"Him being?"

"None other than Quentin Locke."

I waited, not in vain. "And … the manuscript?"

"I have it. He has agreed to relinquish all rights, and for me to hand over the manuscript for a single million."

"He *must* be an Israelite. Is he mad?"

I closed the deal: "Yes. Mad enough to settle for a ten percent discount for cash. This is a one time offer."

"Nine hundred thousand it is. Bring it over now."

"I'm sorry Stephen, but I have to remind you of the hundred thousand finder's fee I am entitled to. It bumps the figure back up to a round million. Are we in, or out?"

The money, or what looked like the money, was on the table in front of Stephen, who predictably unacknowledged my welcome.

"When you have someone at the end of a string – pull don't push," sounded very much like something that the Costas character might have said. Stephen's chronic rudeness was getting to me and, as our relationship was soon to be terminated, I succumbed to an immature urge to give his string a tug or two.

"I know what you're thinking, Stephen. You're wondering if what I have is not some hoo-ha I concocted to pass off as the genuine article. For my part, I am wondering if I should trust *you.* Do I have to count all that money?"

"Here, take it and don't act stupid. Of course it's all there. Who do you think I am? Quick, what have you got for me?"

I opened my attaché case, popped the money in, and poked through its contents. "Now where has it got to?" Dangle, Stephen, dangle. "I'm off to a legal meeting after this. I'm late for it already ... Come on now, where are you hiding? All these papers ... ah yes, got you."

I handed over a computer disk and some papers. "Here it is. I've printed out the next chapter. I've read it and it seems quite good. I hope the rest of it makes the grade and you're not buying a pig in a poke. Click on the drive in your computer and punch in the password ff and enter."

"ff?"

"I don't know. Just 'ff'. Maybe it stands for flim flam? Who knows? Thank you. It's a pleasure doing business with you, but I must rush off now to my next appointment, I'm late as it is ..."

He was already absorbed in the continued adventures of Quentin Locke.

"*Good bye*, Stephen."

No reply. I cut him loose and ran.

## A poignant tale of love-
## *I follow the RPG's instructions and I plan a jailbreak*

The next morning I told my wife that, in my eyes, she was the most exquisite of gems and I could never sully her with presents of inferior diamonds; she told me to eff off.

I ejected myself from between the sheets before the blow landed. My beloved Shrapnelle was slowing down, or maybe in the residual love of the *mikve* morning, she'd found the mercy not to ram her attack home? I was still bamboozled from the dregs of a myriad confusing dreams that had plagued my sleep, so I splashed water on my face in the bathroom sink and focused on myself in the mirror as I brushed my teeth. A busy day was ahead. I had to implement a jailbreak, and I wanted everything to sit in my head in an organized fashion. What I'd learnt the day before at the RPG's was enough to upset anybody's mental applecart.

The RPG had first washed his hands ritualistically, alternating left and right, three times on each side and, with shaking fingers, pressed on the secret catch opening the dreidel's side. Without touching it, he had let whatever was inside slide out onto the table, ever so gently. He turned it over reverently, revealing that both sides of the gold disc were embossed with bumps and ridges. Shiny as the day it was minted.

"What is ...?"

The RPG raised his finger to his lips, signaling silence. He searched the vast religious library covering the walls of his study and found what he was looking for. The chosen books slid out with the ease of constant practice, willing and champing to impart knowledge. He hummed and ha'd, flipping the pages back and forth until he found the references.

He passed the books over to me one at a time, indicating his references while also pointing out additional commentaries, printed both in the margins and as footnotes.

I read, and my throat went dry.

His eyes gleamed, reflecting the holy shimmer radiating from the gold disc that glowed in the dull light of the late afternoon. His voice quavered softly.

"This before us comes from Aaron the Priest's breast plate. It is the *Urrim*. It's the one half. It will be your job, my *boychic*, to get the *Tummin* to complete it. We know where it is. Do you know what this means? If you can get the other half *we can talk with G*d*, as did our Holy Forbears. The *Rebono Shel Olam* (Lord of the Universe) will come down from his *Malhut Shamayim* (Heavenly Kingdom) – to *us*. I must put this treasure safely away."

He carried the *Urrim* over to the shelf and placed it in a silver *etrog*-box. It lay next to a brown, dried-out citron, the jetsam of some Feast of Tabernacles of yesteryear, safely hidden away. Then, as if to reconsider the secureness of the hiding place: “Maybe I should hide it in the Jewish National Fund collection box? No one comes around to empty it anymore. It would be quite safe there, with Zionism being bankrupt in this country ... Or maybe in the spice box?”

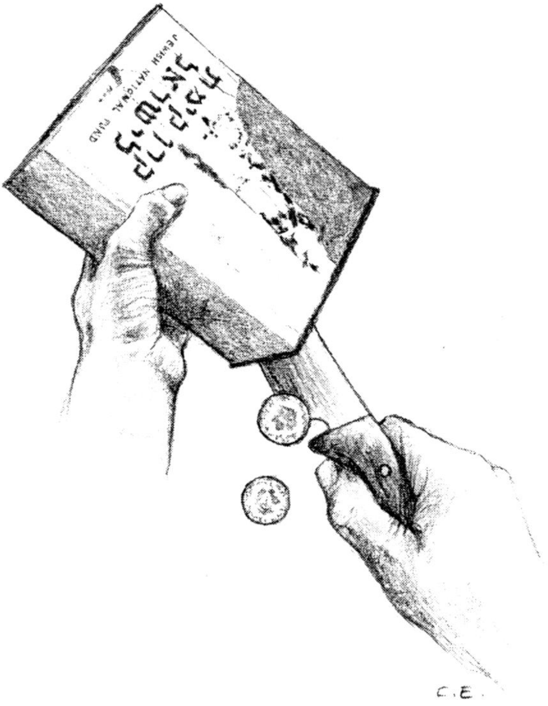

I diverted him from his dilemma. “I’ll have to get a team together. We’re definitely going to need a driver. I’m going to have to spring Duggy from jail. I’m still angry with him for what he did to DuBois, but I can’t let him rot in there forever.”

“*Nu*. And exactly how are you going to arrange that?” The RPG exhibited the interest of someone who had some expertise in such matters.

"I shall go in as Mandrake The Mysterious, Conjuror *extraordinaire* and Master of Magic and Grand Illusion. I will volunteer my services of a full evening of entertaining diversities for the prisoners and wardens."

"*Gevalt!* And what will you come out as – Somebody The Corpse?" was his sarcastic retort, hiding his genuine concern.

Ho, ho.

"Listen to my plan, Rabbi, it may just work. I'll have some assistants all dressed up in ... I don't know exactly what, but I suppose they'll all have matching costumes. I'll start the evening off with some hypnosis. It's good for loosening the atmosphere. I'll select a volunteer from the audience and, after he's been placed deeply under the spell of my hypnotic suggestion, I'll run him through the usual gamut of ridicule. When I count to three and click my fingers, no matter where he is or what he's doing, he'll fall into a deep sleep. I'll have him collapse in a heap onto the stage a few times, like a rag doll. It's always good for a couple of laughs."

"And that volunteer is?" The RPG had guessed it in one.

"Yes Rabbi, it's our man Duggy. He knows what to do and will play along. Acting the loon is an important part of the overall illusion and he's quite good at that and needs no encouragement; he's a natural. Due to his popular success as a hypnotic subject, I'll propose to the audience that I should keep him on stage as my personal assistant for the duration of the show.

"I'll include in the program the Spirit Cabinet Illusion. It'll be the set up for the overall deception. Are you familiar with it?"

"No I'm not. I'm a Rabbi not a vaudevillian."

"It's quite simple, really: I enter a cabinet on the stage and I'm fettered to a chair with the warden's own handcuffs. Hands and feet. Duggy the convict will oversee and supervise. The audience will be relying on him to do a thorough job. This reversal of roles will add much to the entertainment value as Duggy hams it up, probably spoofing one or two of the more popular wardens' idiosyncrasies as he fetters me to the chair.

"Once I'm chained to everyone's satisfaction, my assistants place some musical instruments on the cabinet's floor and Duggy locks me in. After an appropriate pause, from within, the sound of accordions together with the tra-ra of trumpets and the incorrigible Duggy, much to the audience's delight, will unlock and open the cabinet doors, hoping to catch me unawares. Once again the laughter will be at Duggy's expense when I'm discovered, still chained to the chair. Duggy will try repeatedly to catch me out and finally, taking offense at his self-humiliation at not being able to trip me up, and as the holder of the only key to the cabinet, he will refuse to unlock it to let me out. All in the name of getting even.

"The audience will hear me rattling on the walls of the cabinet, as well as my muffled yells, directed at Duggy to open the lock, or else. A magician trapped in his box. Crack-up, crack-up, how amusing.

"You can imagine Duggy's Zulu victory dance, stomping his feet in time with the audience's appreciative chants of 'the Son of Shaka has eaten!', with his tongue sticking out cheekily through the gap in his front teeth and him stabbing the air with his *assegai* key, can't you?"

"No I can't. I'm a Rabbi not an anthro-apologist."

"You are also not a magician, Honored Rabbi, otherwise you would have realized a magician stuck in his own cabinet is an anomaly. No such animal exists. There is more than one way in and out of a spirit cabinet. It was also not *I* who was banging hysterically from within, but one of my assistants, who, hidden from the audience, will be thumping the back of the cabinet from the outside, while shouting into a pillow to muffle his voice. This is the essence of the deception, with the deceived being conditioned to identify a specific sound with a specific action. If all is still hunky dory in Magicland, when the hidden assistant takes to banging the back again, the audience will automatically associate the sound with someone locked in the cabinet. The audience has been set up; the rest is easy."

"Not that what you've done till now seems so difficult."

"Wrong, My Rabbi. I apologize, but the difficult part will be in persuading the Chief Warden to allow the show in the first place."

"*Nu.* So you've got some hard work ahead of you. Make the rest of the story quick; I also have work to do – I have to *doven minche*; it's *shkiya* soon."

"I'll go with you to the *minyan* at the synagogue and we'll talk on the way."

I told him as we hurried along. Of how I would perform the levitation act with Duggy as my assistant and how, when I rip away the cloth covering his floating body, Duggy will have vanished. Now where could he have got to? After the *hauw* of audience appreciation have died down, Duggy will be heard banging around in the locked spirit cabinet, into which he has been magically tele-transported, demanding to be let out.

"The crowd will love this. It'll be Duggy's retribution and with more to come: I will count to three and snap my fingers and Duggy will be heard collapsing onto the floor of the cabinet, to be left there sleeping till the end of the show. The crowd will go wild. Of course it'll be the assistant who'll be doing his bit behind the scenes, banging on the cabinet, not Duggy.

"The master plan is to finish off the evening with a demonstration of metal bending. Probably only spoons, as no knives or forks are allowed in jail. By then, Duggy will be long gone, riding out hidden in the equipment truck on its way ahead of us to set up for the next show."

The Rabbi and I had made it in time to the *minyan*. As

we walked in they had just started the afternoon prayers; *Ashrei yoshvei beitecha,* Praiseworthy are those who dwell in your house ...

"You're over-brushing, Poophead." It was Shrapnelle who had brought me back to reality. "And don't forget deodorant!"

There was my old Luvvy Shrapnelle again – worrying about my hormones. I rinsed and blew in her face for her to check my breath. I was ready for anything the light of the east could throw at me. Go directly to jail, do not pass ...

Chief Warden Archie-bald Hindquarter had an electric chair in his prison office. “It’s not real, you know, but it scares the hell out of the prisoners. I run this prison with psychology you know.”

Every time he said “you know” he peered at me through the thickest of lenses that magnified his watery eyes to the size of black snooker balls. They neither wavered nor blinked. “I’m all for implementing psychology into prison reform. Have a seat.”

I’ll bet you anything you like; nobody, and I mean nobody, ever, ever *thought*, to dare call Archie-bald Hindquarter Bare-Bum Archie.

“I’ve read your proposal and it reads A-okay to me. It seems you must be a busy man, having to rush off afterwards to your next show and all that. It’s a pity. I like magic – it’s all applied psychology you know – and we could have spoken after the show. But let’s see how good you are. Show me a trick. I know what; you can read my mind. I love mental telepathy tricks.”

Part of being a magician is always being prepared and ready for action.

“I have one. It’s called The Lazy Magician’s Card Trick. You’ll like this because at no time do I touch the cards and you do all the work. Think about that! It calls for two decks of cards.” I pulled the decks out my pockets. Having done this trick so many times it felt like *déjà vu.*

“Shuffle them and choose a deck.” He riffle shuffled with a flourish; an amateur with a swank. “Now take out a card. Make sure I can’t see it. Remember it and put it back on the deck. Cut the deck and square up. And another cut, and once more please. Who knows where your chosen card could be now? Not even you. Now look for your card in the other deck and I’ll look through your deck and try to find the card. But first I have to hypnotize you. Look deeply into my eyes ...”

Bare-Bum blinked for the first time. Only once, and

slowly at that. “Are you making fun of me?”

“Huh?”

I galloped through the rest of the trick; found his card. He was astounded, as had been promised in the magic catalogue from which I had ordered the instructions (no special apparatus needed) many years ago with stolen Boy Scout Bob-a-Job money.

“You’re good! The cards must be marked? ... No? Then how did you do it?”

If the price I had to pay to get inside the prison was divulging the secret of my best magic trick, that would be the price I would have to pay. “It’s self-working. When you shuffled the cards I managed to spot what the bottom cards of the decks were, it was especially easy with your fancy riffle shuffle and flourish. All I had to do was to remember that particular card and use it as a marker. For no matter how many times you cut the deck, the card that you chose and put back on top will always be just below it. Cutting doesn’t displace the order of the cards. I look for the master card and your selected card is always next to it.”

“That’s not even psychological – that’s clever. On behalf of the Prison Service I’d like to take you up on your offer of an evening of entertainment.”

The penny must have finally dropped for Stephen when he realized I had never read his mind and he’d been taken in by a three-bob magic trick. How could he have been so stupid? He probably didn’t bother checking to see if the rest of the manuscript was on the disk. He knew it would be empty.

Genesis ch. 37: *And the pit was empty, there was no water in it.*

Rabbinical commentaries: *Why ‘no water’? No water, but snakes and scorpions.*

# EPILOGUE

I had rushed off, both because I *had* to rush off and also because I really was late for my appointment with a certain Shlim Maizel Esq, from Such & Such Publishers Ltd, who, by reply email, had arranged an appointment as requested in my letter to him. Fishing inside my attaché case, I located a copy of that letter and shook out its single fold for a quick run through, just to be sure I had all the facts straight.

*D. RATTELLE & FOULEY & ASSOC.*
*Attorneys at law*
*WILLS & ESTATES*

*Such & Such Publishers Ltd.*

*Dear Sir,*
*Our legal firm has the sad duty of clearing up the Estate of the late Hilliard Cruikshanks.*

*Mr Cruikshanks has set aside a certain sum of money from the legacy that is to be used to finance the publishing of a book from a manuscript he has left behind so as to, 'make a splash after he has gone', as he wrote in his will.*

*Mr Cruikshanks has stipulated in his will that the first printing should be no less than one hundred thousand copies; all at the Estate's expense.*

*One: Does your company have an interest in such an undertaking?*

*Two: Can your company come to an amicable agreement*

*with the Cruikshanks Estate as to how the profits from this venture, if there are to be any, are to be divided up?*

*Please email to arrange an appointment.*

*Yours Faithfully,*
*Fouley. (Attny)*

I arrived. The secretary showed me in.

"Come in, come in. You must be Fouley?" An open-faced man rose to shake my hand.

"Actually, it's Devarin Rattelle, his partner. At the office the secretaries call me Death Rattle behind my back. I suppose it's to be expected – the job description and all. My partner has a bigger problem. There's been a little mishap I'm afraid. It seems that some part of the manuscript has inexplicably disappeared."

"Oh?"

"Here, take this to make a start with the reading." I handed him some papers. "I've searched for the missing bits with no luck – but I think I know a man who can help us."

Once again we were off and running …

**THE END**

מה רבו
מעשיך
ה׳

# HORSERADISH AND JAM

Of the long gone glorious days of my youth that were few and far between, there remain only fond memories.

One can only pine for those annual, lazy, long Easter weekends, which gave singular respite from bilious Monday mornings, when school was put off for a day or two. Memories of picnics by the Van Staden's River Mouth and wading in warm lagoon waters where the aquatic flora squelched murkily between the toes; where, if you were brave and stood in one place long enough, the quicksandy river bottom would suck you down to your ankles and you could daydream about being stuck, trapped, forever a prisoner of a public holiday.

Oh, what fond days those public holidays were.

The Day of the Covenant, re-heralding the Impis' slaughter at Blood River, both by God and *ou Griekie* the canon. And Dingaan's Day, paying tribute to Piet Retief and his party of Boers who were saddled with their just deserts by a party of Zulu slayers on Indaba Hill. All the days of my celebrated freedom, paid for with the blood of others. Indeed, not a bad deal.

But there is one day that was overlooked. A date that has been lost in the annals of history and forgotten by the full belly of time. If it were up to me, we would to this very day all be enjoying an annual long-weekend commemorating Bread Day; participating in a day of loafing and pure leisure.

It was on that momentous day, January 29 1958, when a white government loaf was instituted. Until then everybody ate brown bread. People find it hard to swallow, but believe it or not, all that was available at the grocer's was a brown loaf.

In our house we had a bread cupboard, and my father, who had known the desperation of an empty belly, always insisted that it be kept well stocked with bread and jam, that God forbid no member of his household would ever suffer the ache of hunger.

"Hey Pa, what's to eat? I'm starving!"

Our lot – one of relative affluence and a refrigerator stockpiled with delicacies – the suggested menu would invariably be: "There's bread and jam in the cupboard."

His breakfast of choice was coffee, bread and jam ... as was his supper. And lunch, the main meal of the day, would have been the same had my mother not insisted otherwise. She, a competent cook and a renowned pickler of tongues, claimed Pa had a *meshugas* madness.

As for myself; how I loved that bread cupboard with its extra large *blik* can full of lumpy whole apricot jam, with its savage jagged edges around the open top. One had to risk either tetanus or possibly blood poisoning for the satisfaction of a full belly. But it was well worth it.

Like father, like son.

Once a year, before the Feast of Passover, during which the eating of any leaven is strictly forbidden, Pa would clean out the bread cupboard, tape its door shut, make his way out to the kitchen garden and proceed to dig up a goodly quantity of horseradish. He would announce: "If anyone is hungry, there's horseradish on the kitchen table." (God forbid that anybody should ever go hungry in his house.) Then he would sit down at that selfsame table, place his hands on either side of his head and, rocking backwards and forwards, weep, with the tears rolling down his face, unashamedly.

Ma told everybody it was a *meshugas*. But somehow I knew that there was more to it than meets the eye.

When Aunty Fannie, Pa's sister, stopped by, I asked her about it.

Every family in our community had its thing. Ma's clan was herring and tongue picklers, but from Pa's side it had always been horseradish. It was from him that we inherited our affinity for that powerful root. Be warned; the slightest of nibbles ignites a flame, which bellows up from the belly and volcanoes out via the nostrils, a flame that can only be extinguished with a shot of whiskey. It is also an integral part of the ceremonial Passover Feast and every year the members of our community would come to us for a piece or two of the bitter herb that symbolizes our suffering at the hands of the Egyptians. That was our thing.

So we evacuated ourselves from the house, Aunty Fannie and I. And as we sat there, we two, on the stoep, waiting for the maid, whose face was streaked with tears and snot from the vapors, to finish mincing the horseradish in a manual grinder attached to the kitchen table, Aunty Fannie took my hand in hers and told me about it.

This is our story. The story of our family's collective consciousness, as she told it to me, in her very own words:

"Our family came from Poshvil in Lithuania. Now that may sound like a fancy name to you, but believe me, my boy, there are far, far better places from which to come. Your Granny, my Ma may she rest in peace, was the fourth daughter from a family of five. They eked out a living selling *chrein* – that's horseradish – in the marketplace. The goyim called it dragonroot and used it as a cure-for-all. Somehow they managed to get by and to survive, but you have to sell a lot of dragonroot to afford a dowry, and with so many sisters, well … She was also no beauty queen … Her name was Shayne … Nebech."

She wiped a tear off her cheek with a pink tissue. "The smell of that *chrein* is getting to my eyes, even all the way out here." She excused herself as she gave her nose a good honk.

"And then they heard there weren't enough *maidelach* for the young Jewish men who had left to make their fortunes over here in this place. Letters were written back and forth and one day it arrived; a *skifkaardt* and a letter from your Grandpa, my pa, may he rest in peace. You must understand, my boy, that it was not like today. It was a one-way ticket and she was to leave, never to see her family again. Poor Ma, it must have been very sad for her to leave like that, but it was her only hope for a decent future.

"She packed her few belongings and – all decked out in her

long black velvet Shabbat dress, something totally unsuitable for this climate here, not to mention the heat of a third class cabin in the bowels of a ship – she set out. What is done, is done. Before she left, however, her Ma, my granny, may she rest in peace, gave her daughter a piece of *chrein* which she slipped into her dress pocket. Apparently this was for her to use to combat the seasickness."

I knew what was coming next. In our family we have an expression, 'A pity the railage,' which is used to denote anything that is not worth the candle. No opportunity was ever passed up to enquire of the younger generation: 'A pity the railage'. Do you know where it comes from? And though we have heard the story a thousand times we still listen docilely out of respect and bad habit. I once asked my pa if our family had a predisposition to senile dementia or Alzheimer's. He asked me how he could know such a thing, seeing that everybody in our family had a predisposition to die young. I took the hint and the clip around the ear that came with it.

"In our family we have a saying: 'a pity the railage'. Do you know where it comes from?"

I didn't waste my breath in trying. My Aunty Fannie was on a run. There was no stopping her.

She launched off. "The voyage, in a stifling cabin with four other ladies and no toilet, was terrible. But worse was yet to come. Three weeks later, the boat anchored off East London and she was lowered down over the side in a basket and transported to shore. You must remember that your granny of blessed memory couldn't speak one word of English, and you can imagine how she felt when she was shunted from the boat into a train, with not even a chance of a wash-up." Then she added dramatically, and I mouthed the familiar mantra with her: "Her destination unknown!"

"Hey! Do you know this story? Have you heard it before?"

"Yes, Aunty Fannie – a thousand times."

"Okay then, can you finish it off for me? I'm a bit too teary today." She mopped her nose again with the fragmenting pink tissue.

I felt humbled. This was the first time I had been called upon to finish a family story. Who knows where this could lead. Maybe one day I could start a family story of my own.

So I told Aunty Fannie, leaving out not even one of the 'of blessed memories', how Granny was let off onto the platform at the Humansdorp station. The poor woman – unwashed for weeks with the accompanying odor; hot and sweaty, dressed in a floor-to-ceiling black velvet Shabbat dress, which out of modesty she hadn't removed since having set sail – stood there bedraggled. A no-beauty-queen lost in Afrika.

Two hours later she was found by Grandpa, who was late in coming to town from the Old Farm, still standing on the same spot where she had been deposited. By now there were tears running down her cheeks. The poor, brave woman had finally broken down. She had been too afraid to even move.

But worse was yet to come.

Grandpa was not wise in the ways of etiquette. He approached his bride-to-be, gave her the once over and welcomed her: "A pity the railage!" And Grandma fainted.

She was taken to the farm where her struggles began. There were some happy moments; for example, when she gave birth to my pa and my Aunty Fannie on the kitchen floor, with only an Afrikan lady in attendance.

I knew what Aunty Fannie was going to say, so I said it for her: "And the maid who is now busy grinding in the kitchen is that Afrikan midwife's daughter. Her name was Beauty."

"You're so clever my boy," Aunty Fannie praised me. "A natural storyteller."

Yes indeed – knowing when to hold back in the narrative. I didn't elaborate on the irony that the midwife and my Granny had nothing in common, except that they shared the same name – Beauty and Shayne … Shayne means beauty in Yiddish.

Things were not easy. The desperate hens, pecking for survival, gave themselves up to the Newcastle blight.

Some of the cows were stolen and the rinderpest took the rest.

The hot, slow moving berg wind that had siphoned up its heat off the baked surface of the Little Karoo, deposited its load and desiccated what was left. Like a slow Chinese torture.

And finally, when it eventually did rain, it came down as hail.

The Bluebum Baboon swept down from the krans. A gang of thieves that pogromed the vegetable patch and made off with anything else that was left, including the dog.

"Do you know that I was once nearly kidnapped by the baboons? As a baby, off the front stoep?"

"Please Aunty Fannie, not now. We're reaching the crux of the story."

"Okay my clever boy, but that's the part you don't know. I'll take over the telling."

She told me the impossible – how worse was yet to come. How Granny met the Angel of Death in the kitchen garden. It reared up, dressed in the guise of a black mamba, and struck her on the chest.

"Maybe that was the best that was yet to come. Anyway as far as she was concerned, that is," I whispered.

"That very well may be, my boy. Maybe it was for the best." She cried some more. "Grandpa, my pa may he rest in peace and of blessed memory, was at a loss. There was no Burial Society in the middle of *doer en gone* (far away and still further), so he dressed her in her black velvet Sabbath dress and buried her under the shade of a thorny doringbos tree. Then he took me and your pa, abandoned the old farm, and went to live in Humansdorp.

"It took four years before he managed, with the help of the Burial Society, to go back to the Old Farm and bring her back for a proper burial in a Jewish cemetery.

"Now this is the most amazing thing: the Old Farm was in a terrible mess. The baboons had managed to get into the house and they had ransacked everything. The gardens and fields had been rooted in and had returned to a semi-desert. But … but there was one patch of greenery in that desolate landscape and that was on Granny's grave. That long forgotten piece of horseradish in the pocket of her burial shroud had sprouted and multiplied and, feeding off the fertilizer of Granny's body, had spread lusciously over the grave, protected from the hot sun by the shade of the doringbos. Those damn baboons had turned up their noses at that Lithuanian horseradish. They were no match for it. It was too strong – even for them!

"Grandpa brought some of it back with the body, and it is that which formed the mother lode of our family's horseradish stock. The same stock that your pa digs up every year for *Pesah* – the Passover. And that is why your pa cries over the *chrein.* He somehow believes he's eating his mother. It's the *meshugas* madness."

The wet-faced maid, Beauty's daughter, made an appearance with a prepared jar of minced *chrein* – Jewishness in a Jar – tinted red with the juice of a beetroot. Granny's blood. She presented it to Aunty Fannie with a curtsy.

"Thank you Elizabeth. You're crying. Don't you have a tissue in your pocket? You should always have a tissue in your pocket. Don't you know that? Here – use mine. Keep it."

What is to be learned from this story?

Two things:

One – always have a tissue in your pocket, especially around Aunty Fannie; and two – never ever forget the golden rule of Afrika; always step over a stick lying in the kitchen garden and never step on it, for it may turn into an angry black mamba. Unless you want to end it all, that is.

**THE END**

C.E.

# BANTU BONES

I have been advantaged beyond wildest expectations to be on the receiving end of the most splendid of educations anyone could hope to tolerate in the Halls of Learning. After finishing my bachelors' degree, with hard earned distinctions in psychology and anthropology, I'm presently engaged in attaining an additional honors degree. With little luck and a lot of hard work, I will soon be called upon as Michael InShlanga Bakateeny, with a B.A. Hon. attached to the name.

Attending Professor Charmler's anthropology lecture series was a requisite obligation, being the only BlackMan, peered at openly and smelled at surreptitiously, defined the clammy state of affairs. Compounding the issue was the good professor's disarming habit of finding it necessary to call upon me to help verify his Bantu pronunciations and occasionally, horror of horrors, to consolidate his more esoteric thoughts regarding the *ways* of the BlackMan. I hated being stared at … and smelled out.

And, as claimed the Professor Charmler: "In Afrika, where time has a different nature and many Afrikan languages use the same word for yesterday as for tomorrow, the present is considered the center of time. In Afrikaneese, distance from the present is more significant than direction. As past and future are not differentiated into opposites but, rather, are perceived as more remote forms of the present, this makes the ancestors appear to be real, exerting a profound influence over everyday activities …" It's immaterial from whence I initiate this anecdote, which has many starting points and only one vague ending.

Professor Charmler: "What you say, Michael, old chap? The plural of *ngaka* is *dingaka*?"

"Of course Professor. One, spirit *diviner* – many, *spirit diviners*."

Professor Charmler: "Spirits proliferate in Afrika, as can be expected, and they ply their trade on a plane that is superior to ours, but nevertheless not quite celestial. They are susceptible to a heartening number of very human shortcomings. Some spirits are known to interfere and have to be placated by gifts and sacrifice. Not many have the necessary wherewithal to keep continuous guard. And Africa being Afrika, everyone at some stage or another falls foul of a cantankerous spirit.

"Every Afrikan community boasts *dingaka* who were qualified to act as spirit mediums, whose peacekeeping mission maintains a balance between the different worlds. Most diviners employ some sort of mechanical contrivance. Usually these are sets of bones. Each *ngaka* has an individual collection, but the most treasured aspect of every set is four special tablets made of horn, wood or ivory. When new, they are *blind* and incapable of divining. They have to be left overnight at a nebulous, indecisive locale, such as where mountain tracks intersect. This way they are broken in and geared up to speak."

The professor leaned forward peering over the lectern. Students in the lecture hall felt him engaging their individual attention. An important pearl of information was about to be imparted, judging by the professor's look.

"Does anyone know what a hypnogogic illusion is?" And so a question.

As a psychology major, I had been wondering when that question would eventually pop up.

"Michael, this is your expertise. Perhaps a little enlightenment on your part? Fill us all in, please."

I filled them in. "An example of such an illusion is when you hear the alarm clock ringing at exactly seven o'clock, even though you haven't set it, because you normally get up at that hour. Or perhaps, supposedly the phone rings and you rush to answer and end up talking to a dialing tone. Or hearing your children's voices when they are away at summer camp and you are missing them …"

Charmler went through his peering-over-the-podium-at-us act again. A lateral form of *déjà vu* to be sure – similar circumstances, only a different ectoplasmic question. "So then, maybe they smoke too much *dagga?* Perhaps the divining *dingaka* hear things that aren't really there?

"I once met a real *ngaka*. Had a long chat with him. Even fed me an exotic meal, he did. Stewed Guinea Fowl it was, with a shared bottle of warm Lion Lager. Most enjoyable."

Now *that* was interesting. No one in their right mind would dish up stewed Guinea Fowl to anybody – it's disgusting. Road-kill would be better served. Something was up.

Ensconcing himself more comfortably on the lectern, his throne of learning, he professored on. "Here's an anecdote from our little get together. It's a story the *ngaka* told me. *I* call it *Practical Psychology the Bantu Way*:

"Apparently one of the chief's goats skipped town, so to speak. The entrails were found close by in the bush and evidently the culprit was a hungry local. Our diviner was called in, threw his bones and declared that a chicken had been an eyewitness to the crime. Now, as we know, chickens can't talk, but undeterred, my *ngaka* friend placed the chicken in a cast iron cooking pot that stood over the ashes. He told them that it was bound to recognize the guilty party's touch and would let out an accusing squawk.

"Each villager had to touch the pot gently. All went through the rigmarole, but with no squawk from the chicken.

"Still undeterred our canny diviner lined up all the villagers and looked at the palms of their hands for soot. All had soot-covered hands except for the culprit, who, afraid of the consequences, had only pretended to touch the cooking pot."

I couldn't help myself. I broke the story's aftermath with a low Bantu laugh that welled up surreptitiously from within. A laugh much removed from the WhiteMan's Guinea Fowl-cackle as it rolled out, belly deep in gentle guffaw; a non-specific disquieting sound.

"Michael – you asthmatic?"

Someone had been pulling professor Charmler's chain, and I had an inkling as to his identity. There was only one *ngaka* capable of stirring up such a ridiculous story, such imaginative hyena droppings – and back the whole caboodle up with a Guinea Fowl dinner. It could only be Uncle Old Man Bakateeny.

I couldn't suppress more laughter, but it was not *I* this time, for Old Man's spirit had entered me. Years ago he had laughed behind the professor's back, now again laughter, this time in his face. I, his sounding board. My uncle may have been the one to pull the professor's chain then, but it was my honors degree he was flushing down the toilet now.

I only think it was me, for my voice lost its affected halls of learning nasality and took on a Bantu-esque throatiness. "The Zulu have an expression for a stupid person: he who urinates into the wind. And you, my *ProfessorChief*, seem to have splashed your trouser cuffs." He looked down, examining his trousers. "And that's why we wear loincloths."

Continuing: "You are wrong in every aspect, *for you are like the baboon who can only count to three*, and it is difficult for me to know where to begin. First things first: The *dingaka* are aware of hypnogogic illusions and *that* is why they use the bones. They don't need the bones to talk to the spirits. They only need them after, to verify what they heard was indeed spiritual and not hypnogogic echoes. The 'diviner and the chicken' story has no essence, as the spirits could have directly pointed to the culprit without any additional dung-patties fed to hungry professors, who eat like the hyena and run off science instead of art.

"I'll tell a story that will elucidate. So be like the buffalo who listens to the tickbird. I call it *The Tapiologist*.

"There are still *dingaka*. In the townships you'll find them. Also in the mines and jails. Some are out there in Afrika, alone in the bush chatting online with the spirits. Old Man Bakateeny was one of those. He worked, keeping heart and soul together, for the South African Railways.

"The railway line started in Northern Rhodesia, boiled its way through Bechuanaland, crossed the border near Mafeking and swung around to Kuruman before winding its way through Southern Afrika. Its final destination, the Port Elizabeth docks.

"There is no more middle-of-nowhere than the Kalahari, and it was on the edge of this desert, one hundred and thirty miles north of Kuruman, where Old Man Bakateeny – in his spare time tending his modest *dagga* plantation – was stationed. He was in charge of Map Point 18. His job description: Tapiologist. His issued equipment: one set of work overalls and an iron rod. He was there for three years.

"From the Rhodesian mines they came, more than a hundred carriages long, filled with red manganese and black iron ore. With two powerhouse diesels in front and one at the back, those trains trundled along at a steady pace. Once moving, inertia took hold and nothing could stop them. And if the drivers forgot to begin braking from at least fifty miles outside of Port Elizabeth, the train would eventually be halted only as it sank into the Indian Ocean.

"A BantuMan feels at ease and not in the least bit underdressed as long as his prepuce cover – generally a small round dried gourd – is safely attached. It was only every second day that Old Man Bakateeny donned his work overalls and waited for the scheduled ore-train to pass him by.

"Iron rod in hand, it was his responsibility to tap each and every wheel of the carriages as they went by, listening to the ping sound of the strike; checking the wheels' fidelity by their resonance. If a wheel had a crack, a potentially disastrous situation that threatened derailment, then the sound supposedly would be different.

"He was a bit hazy as to what that different sound was supposed to be or what he should do if he ever heard it. Perhaps too much *dagga* had taken its toll, for all he could remember of his ten minute training session in the Kuruman shunting yards before he was dropped off at Map Point 18 was: "If you damage that iron rod in any way, I'll take a sjambok to you!"

"The seasons passed and, like clockwork, our resident Tapiologist was at his post, squatting alongside the track … tap-ping … tap-ping … tap-ping … tap-ping … an exercise in monotonous concentration as those rolling xylophones were more than a mile long … tap-ping … tap-ping … tap-ping …

"… Then one day … a tap-PONG …

"The rod dropped from Old Man Bakateeny's hand. He had heard a PONG, that was for sure. Quick thinking was not the issue, as there was plenty of time before the last diesel engine would pass him by. He turned over slowly the multi-situation with its apparent consequences:

"One: if it was the spirits, what was he to understand from their message; or two: if a hypnogogic experience, then perhaps he should cut back on his *dagga* pipe; but if three: the wheel *was* cracked, maybe he should at least wave frantically at the last diesel engine's driver in an effort to stop the giant rolling millipede before it attempted the squealing descent down DoodMansKloof Pass, whose straining gradient would certainly shatter the cracked wheel and send the whole bangtoot lurching unimpeded over the precipitous edge, causing untold damage and injury?

"There was only one way to ascertain for certain, and that was to ask the bones.

"He took the bag hanging from his neck and opened it. Working loose the *riempie*-thong he raised it to his lips and blew into it, breathing life into the bones …

*'My moon-coloured blood-brothers I swallow-suckled you from black-purple teats. And black and white kraaled heifers whom I herded as a picaneen. Be aware that this is of my old fathers' tradition. All* dingaka *they were. This is not a witch's dream. Not sucked from a dry gourd. So be of aid ... see truths.'*

"Then he threw the bones …"

**THE END**

C.E.

# AUTHOR'S NOTE

Over the years, with encouragement from people whose advice I follow, namely that I write things down, I had developed into something of a storyteller. Dinnertime presented an opportune moment to both enrich and sate the family's cultural appetite with my literary endeavors.

After the maid cleared all unchewable debris from the table, I harrumphed theatrically so all present – Ma and Pa – would stop verbal arm wrestling over who knows what and settle down to be highly entertained by my modest pencillings.

I began to read: "Let sleeping dogs lie … by yours truly."

The work became this short story … I still weep when I read it.

***Daniel Abelman***

# KADDISH

*Lord Field Marshal Montgomery's order of the day before the crucial battle of el Alamein in the Second World War: We are going to knock the Jerry out of Africa for a six.*

The slowness of the day's activities belied what was in store. The gunpowder had been made – enough to fill an empty litre Coke bottle. After numerous failed attempts at detonation – each one a dance with death – the mixture was deemed impure by the experts and the burnt-out boxes of matches were used as kindling to start a fire on the garage floor. Maybe, just maybe, there would be enough flame to set the whole thing off.

No such luck.

The boys chucked the dud into the dying embers and, giving up on the project, moved onto the next activity of the day – torturing the dog. But not for too long as it was a lazy beast, and when the boys had untied his back leg (could a dog jump over burning embers on three feet?), he walked around in ever decreasing circles and flopped down with a grunt onto his flattened area of the garage floor. Curled up, with his nose snuggled into his rear end and after a satisfied sigh, obviously enjoying his own earthy pungency, the canine insulated himself from the outside with his tail over his head and settled down for a nap until suppertime.

The boys voted on another inning of cricket on the front lawn until suppertime – thank the Lord – because that's when it exploded.

There was a hell of a bang followed by a strange silence that was broken by the ee-awe-ee-awe of the emergency vehicles' sirens. The doves on the surrounding rooftops had hardly fluttered back to their corrugated iron perches before a gang of shaken boys took off; they were hightailing it for the hills. Some didn't build up enough courage to come home for days, and legend has it that one or two of them might very well still be way up in them there mountains.

Monty would have been proud of them. Those boys had knocked that garage out of Africa for a six!

The dog, who had had his nose blasted up his bum, was the only victim. His remains were buried in the driveway, forever at rest under the cool shade of a spreading marula tree – the poor beast.

The end.

Ma said: "What rubbish!" And Pa said: "Why all of this? Let's hear the rest of it." Pa was astute. "Spit it out," was his order of the day.

I hawked up the triumvirate of errors that was clogging me and spat it out. "Three things went wrong – and they weren't my fault."

My opening gambit of denial was declined. Ma pressure-pinched the bridge of her nose, attempting to numb her frontal lobe to what was coming next, while Pa, he just grinned.

"Well – the legend that some of the boys are still up there in those them mountains is not exactly a legend. The thing is – it's true, because I buried one of those boys up there in the bush. With my own hands."

Ma said: "Such utter rubbish!" And Pa. Well, Pa just stopped grinning.

The first of the three errors was indisputably Harelip Wally's fault. It's still an open question as to what was going through Wally's head; and any theory put forward could be considered true, unless proven otherwise. Of course, Wally blames DoffNoontjie, his dolly-bird, for the whole thing. "If only you would've let me touch you inside your shirt," he had complained to her afterwards.

Wally had a point: It was in all probability the broken stop-cock on his testosteronal overflow that precipitated down his foot and pushed the accelerator pedal in direct disregard for the warning signs along the roadside advertising danger. Wally had been swanking just a *leetle* bit too much at the wheel of the extra heavy No. 2 fire engine he had just been promoted to – and was sitting behind for the first time.

"Wait till DoffNoontjie hears about this promotion," he addressed his hard on. It was action this day for Wally: he had heard all about the urban terrorists who were waiting to strike, and when the alarm came in about an explosion, he was raring to go. He already felt part of the anti-terrorist squad that was going into action for the very first time.

"DoffNoontjie is going to loosen up when she hears about this," his hard on replied.

We are not exactly talking about what could be termed 'high intelligence' when it came to Leading Fireman Wally and his Prospective. An ardent jukskei player was our Wally – she had even allowed him a kiss when his team was runner up in the over-21 section at the Easter Show – and he knew nothing about croquet. So he never could fully appreciate the beauty of the back swing of his red fire truck as it tonked the brown Beetle that was vrooming up the Slagtersnek Kloof road in the oncoming direction; for like a croquet hammer striking at a ball, that brown Beetle spun over the edge and bungee jumped, floating in slow motion, down, down into the torrential waters of Slagtersnek River far below.

The fire-engine careened out of control as Wally fought the wheel, finally coming to a standstill, but not before it trampled what used to be a sign that once read 'remain in low gear at all times!'

In one fell swoop he had wiped out the whole Freckleton Clan: Fluffy Freckleton the boy, and his parents, Mr and Mr Fluffy. All Harelip Wally could manage at that time was a whispered: "Yirre fokken Yissus man."

Pa said: "Don't swear boy." And Ma said: "Mrs Fluffy?" and started giggling.

Of course, her real name wasn't Mrs Fluffy. It was Aunty Bubbles. Up to a certain age all adult females are referred to as Aunty this or Aunty that. Then, as the local custom still dictates, all friends' parents were given the first names of their sons. Hence: Mrs Fluffy. We couldn't very well have called her Mrs Freckleton, as she was the genetic carrier of Fluffy's complexion, now could we? It was strange how fitting the names the parents were given really were. Hence Ma's giggles.

Getting on with it, I told Ma: "Mrs Fluffy Freckleton is the crown bearer of the second 'thing that went wrong'."

The mistake was that she sat in the back seat of the Beetle. She claimed she felt safer that way, and it was probably true, as Mr Fluffy, her cute hubby, was a habitual wife beater, ruthlessly abusing her both physically and verbally. In the back seat of the Beetle, she was out of striking range.

He was adjusting the rear view mirror, playing with it, trying to snare her reflection as to witness the hurt of his verbal stings. He had just enquired in spotty jest if a cow with diarrhoea had farted in her face when she was a child, when Wally in his red No. 2 fire engine swung round the bend from the opposite direction and came straight for them. Maybe, and only just maybe, the cute Mr Fluffy could have avoided that red stampede had he kept his eyes on the road. Speculation aside, the outcome was only Mrs Fluffy's body was recovered, trapped the way it was in the back seat. The bodies in the front were never found and presumed washed out to sea, to be nibbled away by tomorrow's catch.

"So it's two down, one to go," said Pa. "And I speculate the third thing that went wrong has a little bit more to do with you, my boy. Right or wrong?"

So as not to speak ill of the dead and buried as they never can pay the piper for their misdeeds, at least not in this world, and knowing someone would have to pay the price for what went wrong no matter what, I blamed it all on Old Man Bakateeny and hoped for the best.

"It was Old Man Bakateeny's idea – the whole thing."

Ma said: "What unadulterated rubbish!" And Pa, he just started grinning again, enjoying the chase after the ultimate truth.

It was Old Man Bakateeny who had put me up to it. He told me about rocky spots up in the mountains that were a favorite with the puff adders, who basked the days lazily away in the hot sun and were an easy catch. He also gave detailed instructions on how to trap these not so accommodating creatures. He planned for me to live off the land for three weeks as part of my initiation into Afrikan manhood. I planned for one day, or a day and a half – max.

On our road trips through the countryside it was not uncommon to see a child of Afrika participating in such initiations. It was demanded of them that they should wander off into the bush and live off the land. They were forbidden any contact with other persons and their faces were painted an oval white as a warning not to approach them. Living off the land certainly left them with plenty of spare time on their hands. In the middle of nowhere they could be seen standing motionless at the edge of the bush-line watching the occasional speeding car pass them by. The culmination of this initiation right was a circumcision ceremony traditionally utilizing an unexpectedly sharp edge of a dried sugar-cane leaf and the end of a penis.

Pa said: "Lucky for you, you're Jewish, my boy. Old Man Bakateeny's hand is not as steady as it used to be." And Ma said: "You mean you ate puff adders? Total rubbish!"

"No Ma, of course not. I sold them to the Snake Park. They milk them for their venom. They pay for them by the inch."

It was on the same afternoon the news came through on the local radio about the Slagtersnek Kloof road tragedy that I ascended through the bush into the mountains with my snake prospecting equipment; two broomsticks and an old kitbag. As I made my way, circumnavigating clusters of thorn bushes and the even more impregnable clumps of aloes, I replayed Old Man Bakateeny's virtual reality demonstration on how to hunt serpents, with his leather belt, black with age and grime, starring as the snake and his fingers forked out, cast as two broomsticks with double pronged wooden forks firmly attached to their ends. He raised a lot of dust with his production, and for a while the belt was indeed morphosized into an angry adder as he danced and parried, wove and ducked; and finally outwitting the reptile, he, with a Bantu victory cry – *Inshlinga*, I have eaten – trapped it to the ground, pinning it with his forked fingers as it squirmed, frantically trying to escape.

We went through all the variations. We did puff adders, boomslangs, mambas and touched on the ringhals cobra. There is no bottom line with snakes; each and every kind should be approached according to its specific shape and temperament. But never, never be so stupid as to try and grab a snake from behind the head – the end with the worn brass buckle – you'll be stuck with angry death clamped in a curl around your wrist. Always, after firmly planting the snake to the ground with one forked stick behind the head and the other further down the body, grab it by the tail. Apparently, if you hold it upside down and continually bob the creature up and down with a gentle yo-yo action, it can't whip back up and sink its fangs into your hand. Anyway, that's the way it worked with the belt.

Boomslangs or tree snakes are back-fanged and they can only inflict any real damage if they can get hold of extremities like your nose or fingers. Mambas are gentle and will glide away unless you accidentally step on them. Adders are trickier than others because their bodies are fat around the midriff and thin around the neck and the females hardly have any tail at all. And the cobra is difficult both because of its aggressive nature and the neck, which is difficult to pin down as it rears up when threatened. Let's not forget it can spit venom into your eyes with blinding accuracy. If you do perchance come across a cobra – walk away, tough guy, just walk away!

Basically what Old Man Bakateeny trained me to do during that afternoon we spent together, was to grab the thing by the tail and pop it head first into the kitbag. He insisted that the hand is faster than a striking snake and, except perhaps for the black mamba, one can jerk the hand away in time. I had quickly got the hang of it after my instructor and master fetched me a couple of hard raps on the knuckles with his belt buckle.

I made a fire and mixed the white ashes with clay, as per instructions, to prepare a gritty paste for my face.

With a broomstick casting for snakes, I was making my way up a donga when from the other direction appeared what could only have been a ghost. I was trapped within the red earthen walls of the washed out gully and, to make matters worse, so was the ghost. The hairs at the nape of my neck rose and I could feel the blood sinking to my feet, freezing them in place as the spectre and I faced off, one opposite the other.

Many strange stories have come out of the Afrikan bush. Far from humans, the forces of the *sitre ahra* are the true guardians of the continent, but never before has it been heard that two separate apparitions somehow managed, with all those wide expanses available to them, to bump into each other unexpectedly and in doing so, scaring the living daylights out of each other.

It was the ghost of Fluffy Freckleton. The phantom ghoul looked at me in the most horrible of ways and began to wail and moan, venting the anguish of his death. Maybe it was a banshee for all I knew. And then it spoke to me: "What are you doing here?"

Fear edited my answer: "Living on the land – an initiation rite – catching snakes."

"So that's that white stuff on your face then. Heck man, you really scared me. You heard how I screamed. I really thought that you were a ghost or something."

It wasn't a ghost and it wasn't a banshee. What it was, was an alive and still breathing Fluffy Freckleton. Somewhere along the line, somebody seemed to have slipped up – made a mistake of sorts. We sat down in the donga – our knees still a bit shaky.

He told me how they had *exploded* the garage and how he was too scared to go home because his father would *donner* the living daylights out of him.

"Check it out," he said. "I'll do the initiation rights with you. That way we can keep company together. Hey, they won't have to clip us, will they?"

"No way, Fluffy. It's already been taken care of. We're Jewish."

"Thank God!" he said.

How could I tell the poor boy both his parents were dead and everyone had legitimately presumed he had been with them in the car? I would keep him with me for a day or two before leading him out of the bush to face orphancy.

We hunted snakes together, two friends alone in the veldt.

Then we struck pay dirt – it was a beautiful adult green mamba. Not as common as his black cousin but twice as poisonous. The most venomous snake in the world would fetch a pretty price at the Snake Park. It would keep two hungry lads who were living off the land in Burger Kings for a month.

Ma said: "I don't believe any of this. How much do they pay for a green mamba in its prime?" And Pa said: "It's in the measure of things. Everything we do has to be measured."

Pa must have been telepathic, for he had hit the nail, and the third and final error, on the head; for it was indeed all in the measure of things.

Fluffy made a grab for the tail while I went for the kitbag. Do the arithmetic. Fluffy was four feet and five inches tall. The snake was five foot nine long – too long. There was too much of the dangling mamba left on the ground. It rose up and bit poor Fluffy on the calf. Twenty minutes later that stupid, stupid boy was dead.

"I couldn't very well drag him all the way out of the bush, it was just too far, and to leave him there to swell up in the heat … so I buried him. On the way down I realized he was already dead somewhere else and no one would miss him. I left him there and till now I've told nobody."

Ma said: "If any part of this hogwash is true, which is highly unlikely, why are you telling us now?"

"Fluffy should be buried in a Jewish cemetery, that's why."

The next day Pa went off to have a long talk with a Rabbi from the old country. He stopped in at the Regional Council Surveyors Office and bought a two acre morgen of Afrika. A rocky plot, a serpent-ridden Eden high up where the spirits roam, there is where Fluffy rests, in the only one-man Jewish cemetery in the world.

Once a year we still climb up there, on the anniversary of his passing, to say Kaddish – the prayer for the dead.

**THE END**

Catherine Edmunds worked for two decades as a classical musician before switching careers to re-invent herself as an artist/illustrator and author. Her artwork embraces such diverse themes as delicate portraiture and exploding beetroots. Recent publications include cover art for Earlyworks Press. Catherine's writing is embedded in the natural world and veers between fantasy and romance with a dash of humour. "woomword, earth and honey", her first solo poetry collection, will be published in 2008 by Circaidy Gregory Press. Catherine is married with three children and lives in North East England between the grey North Sea and the windswept high Pennines.

Daniel Abelman's youth was spent wandering the southern reaches of the Dark Continent, absorbing a diversity of languages, cultures and experiences whilst visiting friends in the most incongruous of places; or just living off the land.

Born in Port Elizabeth, South Africa, his childhood – spent in a backyard swarming with grasshoppers and overrun with chickens – was interrupted when he was given a pair of black lace-up shoes and sent off to school. Years later, after miserably failing his matriculation exams, he was given a long pair of pants and sent out to seek his fortune in the big wide world.

Quickly learning how to evade ticket inspectors on trains, he was soon a mobile up-and-coming young man with a bright future. He has since seen-it-and-done-it, as can be attested to by his checkered curriculums vitae: snake-hunter; soldier; tightrope walker; magician; restaurant/bar manager; hypnotist and peeker into things people seldom or never see … or in some cases never imagined to exist.

Having won a stake in a card game, he flew to Europe. When he found the climate too cold, he made his way to the Levant where he now lives. Jerusalem, where he married a rabbi's daughter and is the proud father of four children, is now his permanent base.

**Also published by BeWrite Books**

**As the Crow Flies**
**by Dave Hutchinson**

Colonists struggle to terraform Mars … a seedy psychiatrist finds himself locked in combat with a psychopath … sightseeing aliens decide to visit one of the worst places on Earth … a teacher's past catches up with him in an unimaginable way … and a Special Forces assassin finds a bizarre kind of redemption in an English wood.

Only five of the fifteen short stories in this collection to challenge the reader and stretch imagination to the limits.

*... it's time for more readers to discover Hutchinson's imaginative stories for themselves.* **Ellen Datlow**

**ISBN** 978-1-904492-23-8

## Also published by BeWrite Books

### The Hundredfold Problem
### by John Grant

The story begins several million years ago, when sentient machines from an alien civilization build a Dyson Sphere around the sun's Red Dwarf companion star (which is why we've never seen it) and seed the Sphere with Neanderthals …

Or maybe it begins in the future, after terrestrial humanity has discovered the Sphere (now called the Big Dunkin Donut), colonized it, and enslaved the natives.

Whatever … the Donut is in peril.

Atheist fundamentalist preachers – Rev Rick "The Man" Hamfist and Rev Bo "No Messin" Fingers – inspired by dastardly Dennis the Complete Bloody Sadist, are waging an evangelical war there with the aim of destroying the local, very real, goddess LoChi.

Using a matter transmitter, Earth sends holochips of two plucky adventurers to sort this out: heavy-weapons-toting xeno-anthropologist and scantily clad babe Petula McTavish; and by-the-rules supercop Dave Knuckle. But Knuckle's holochip is accidentally shattered on arrival into one hundred fragments, which are reconstituted to form one hundred lethally diverse partial versions of the supercop.

McTavish now has a hundredfold problem to solve. Actually a one-hundred-and-one-fold problem, but that wouldn't have made as good a title.

And that's before she falls in love …

*The Hundredfold Problem* is that rarest of things – a gloriously funny romp, populated by outrageous, larger-than-life characters, that's also an extremely imaginative, challenging sf novel.

**ISBN** 978-1-904224-49-5

www.bewrite.net

## Also published by BeWrite Books

### The Bad Seed
### by Maurilia Meehan

Her young daughter has disappeared, sparking a massive murder hunt, and now her husband has gone walkabout in the bush with no plans to return.

Nothing is coming up roses for small-time gardening correspondent Agatha.

So she plants the seeds of a new life in an isolated village … in the dilapidated former home of a renowned witch.

A strange new lover and mysterious visitors from half a world away will not allow Agatha's own ghosts to rest … and her garden produces dark honey and poison as Maurilia Meehan's tale builds to a chilling climax.

Sinister flora and phantoms flourish in this rich and unforgettable work from the pen of the award-winning author of the acclaimed "Performances", "Adultery", "The Sea People" and "Fury".

**ISBN** 978-1-905202-12-6

www.bewrite.net

## Also published by BeWrite Books

### The End of Science Fiction
### by Sam Smith

**No matter how important your job ... would YOU turn up for work knowing that you and every living being on the planet will be dead before pay day?**

A beautiful young woman is brutally murdered – just as governments around the world announce that the universe will end in five days' time.

The planet Earth's 6.5 billion human beings deal with their impending extinction in 6.5 billion ways. But amid global chaos, dedicated detective Herbie Watkins stays on the case, determined to discover the killer against a merciless clock that's ticking away his own final hours.

Is he insanely obsessed, or is he the last sane man in the history of the human race?

Sam Smith weaves a unique cop story of a unique cop against a unique backdrop in a unique page-turner of a book.

No count-down novel, no disaster book, no police saga has ever been written to thrill the reader and plumb the depths of the human soul as does The End of Science Fiction. It is the last word in SF and crime … and much more.

You will read The End of Science Fiction over and over again, asking new and challenging questions of yourself and formulating new answers every time you re-open this outstanding work from the pen of an author who demands one-sitting novel reading.

**ISBN** 978-1-904492-70-2

www.bewrite.net

Printed in the United Kingdom
by Lightning Source UK Ltd.
131050UK00002B/46-69/P

9 781905 202287